shifting the mind's eye

Barbara S. Carr

ISBN: 978-0-473-55108-7
Taiharuru Press, taiharuru.co.nz

Barbara S. Carr

Thank you for your thoughtfulness and encouragement

Zac Miller-Waugh
Odette Miller
Kevin Waugh
Travis Bull
Sue Webster
Leasy DeLong

Lots of Love
Barbara

Cover Painting: Flowers on Show by Patricia Brickell
patriciabrickell@icloud.com

Contents

The Price of a Virtuous Woman

Mum and me are down with the chooks. 'We need to find some eggs,' Mum says. 'We've only got a shilling to last 'til I get the pension.' Mum is feeding them the vegie scraps—today it's mostly pumpkin skin and grey mashed potato. I start pulling strips of bark off the gum tree so they can eat the slaters hiding underneath. They love slaters better than wheat I reckon. Mum says they eat too much wheat anyway and don't lay enough eggs to earn their keep. "What you want to do is put them in the pot," Mr Ramsbottom said. I laughed like mad when Mum told me his name. Ramsbottom! The butcher! But Mum clouted me so I don't do it anymore. Anyway, who's going to chop the chooks' heads off? Not us. Not likely.

The gum tree bark is thick and powdery and I wriggle my fingers underneath and haul off another strip. The slaters try to escape away but I run with the bark into the chook yard. I yell, 'Chook, chook, chook,' and the hens come running up with Brownie in the lead. She's the fattest shiniest hen. Mum thinks she might be eating eggs and that's why she looks so good. While Brownie pecks at the slaters and other hens, I stroke her feathers and even touch her knobbly red comb.

Soon the slaters have gone and Brownie leaves for the gum tree. It's a huge tree. A branch came off in the storm last week. The leaves on it still smell good. I crunch some and sniff like mad and then the sun comes out and it's hot. The sun shines on the stripped trunk of the tree and I can see a ruby, hard and small but shining, shining… and another and another. They are everywhere—in the cracks of the bark and weeping straight out of the trunk. I carefully pick them up and put them in the old baked bean tin I have in my hut in the bamboo. Looking through the big ones is not the same as looking through red cellophane. I see a little bit of red like the last of the fire.

'Come on slow-coach! You haven't got the eggs yet and we have to pick the butterbeans as well.'

I hide the rubies in the hut. Then look for eggs. It's hard because the hens lay their eggs any old where and sometimes I don't find them until too late. I get two. Mum frowns.

'Is that all? Well that settles that then. We'll have to go to the shop.' I like the shop. Mr Purdie sometimes gives me a bit of cheese or a jellybean. He lets me pick the jellybean right out of the jar and I always pick a red one. I like his white apron and the big shiny knife he cuts the cheese with. I like the smell of the shop. I like the packets on the shelves and the silver scales he weighs the cheese on. When I am lucky Mum lets me have the chair by the counter and she says 'Don't kick the counter, or you'll have to get down' and I don't kick the counter. Of course, if a lady comes in I get down.

We get ready to go and Mum puts on her green coat with the little furry bits in the collar. She powders her face (when she says she is going to powder her nose she goes to the toilet instead). Then she puts red lipstick on out of a little golden tube and pushes her lips together and she brushes her hair. She looks beautiful. The mirror in the bathroom is broken but she can still see herself in it. Mr Ramsbottom said: "What you want to do is get rid of that old mirror and put a decent one in." Mr Ramsbottom leans over the fence when Mum is in the garden and talks. He says, "What you want to do is plant your beans now and what you want to do is get some firewood ready for the winter so's it will have time to dry and what you want to do is get a man in to fix that window..." Sometimes he pops in for a cup of tea. He's got one leg cut off and one day I got under the table and his real leg was bent but the other one stuck straight out in front of him and I touched it! It was made of iron like our beds and it had a rubber bit on the end like our beds as well. People say "He lost it in the war you know" and their voices sort of whisper as if it's a secret. That's silly -- you can see there's no foot.

Mr Ramsbottom brought a whole roast of beef for us one day—with sticks all through it and string and it was so big it would have lasted for days and Mum said she couldn't take it because she couldn't pay for it and wouldn't have charity. Mr Ramsbottom said, 'Well that was all right it was for me'. I said 'Mum says we've only got one shilling until pension day' -- but Mum said to hush so I did. And Mr Ramsbottom ended up wrapping the roast in the newspaper and carrying it away under his arm.

I wish we could have kept the roast but I don't much like Mr Ramsbottom's shop. It smells. Only the sawdust on the floor behind the counter where he chops the meat is good. I can make patterns with my toes. What I don't like is him wiping the blood off his hands onto his stripy apron -- and the choppers are scary.

'Wake up dreamy,' Mum says. She picks up the basket. It is square and has a shiny green line on it that looks the same as the coat.

It isn't far to the shop. The footpath is horrid now. It used to be smooth and black and you could run on it and squash the puddles when it rained. Then they fixed all the holes and put sharp red stones on it—just because the Queen is coming to visit Mum says. I ask if she is coming to our street and Mum just laughs. We go past Mrs Turner's house and she is at the gate looking into her letterbox. Mum stops and asks how she is.

'As well as can be expected Mrs Monro.' But she has purple lips. Purple. And her friend Mary does her shopping with her because she is sick and Mary has to put pills into Mrs Turner's mouth if she falls down. Mary hates doing the shopping with Mrs Turner. She is scared she will fall down.

We go past Mr Davie's house and his dog barks at us. Then we're at the shop. As we go in and the bell on the door rings I breathe in as much as I can. You can't breathe in forever. Mrs Ramsbottom is on the chair. She is telling Mr Purdie what she wants: 'I'll have a pound of your best cheddar, and a half pound of tea—not the stuff you sent me last time. It was full of dust and Mr Ramsbottom won't take tea with dust in it….' Her mouth curls and sneers like a witch. Her b-t-m is too big for the chair. She is wearing a black coat over a black frock and her back is lumpy—as if she has been tied tightly in the middle but the top of her back has escaped. Grandma looks like that. She wears a pink corset with pink shoelaces in it. Well, they mightn't be shoelaces but they look like them. Mum's back is smooth. She doesn't wear a corset. Mrs Ramsbottom's hands are fat too and she has lots of rings on them. She is holding onto her black bag tightly and diamonds and rubies and gold poke out from her fingers. Her rubies are shinier than mine. Mrs Turner said to Mum that if Mrs Ramsbottom died they'd have to cut the rings off. I look at the rings. I see blood all over her hands and don't want to look any more.

'Good morning Mrs Ramsbottom,' Mum says and Mrs Ramsbottom nods at her and carries on with her list.

'Get the boy to deliver it this afternoon at two,' she says. 'I'll take the tea with me now.' I look at the grocer's bike outside the shop. I want a bike. Not one with a huge basket on it though. Shiny black would be nice. Mr Purdie gets a paper bag and starts getting tea out of the box.

Mrs Ramsbottom slides off the chair and looks at Mum. 'I always think lipstick looks cheap Mrs Monro', she says firmly, then takes the tea from Mr Purdie and waddles out of the shop to sit on the seat outside. Mum laughs.

Mr Purdie doesn't laugh. He looks unhappy.

'I'll have some tea, a quarter of a pound, and half a pound of cheese, Mr Purdie,' Mum starts. Mr Purdie shakes his head sadly.

'I can't,' he whispers. 'Not unless you could see your way to clearing the slate Mrs Monro.' What does that mean? I have a slate at school but soon I will be allowed to print on paper. What does Mum have to do?

Mum has gone red. 'The widow's benefit is next Tuesday Mr Purdie. I will pay then.'

'I'm sorry,' he says. 'Every month you pay some — but not all. And it has gone on too long and the debt is growing. I am truly sorry but unless you can see your way to completely paying what you owe...' Mr Purdie looks at the floor and his hands hold each other in front of the white apron. My Mum looks up at the roof and she looks as if she is going to cry. Mr Purdie looks as if he is going to cry too. Then Mum kind of sticks her chin out and says she will sort it out somehow and picks up the basket and we go outside.

'I'm just waiting for Mr Ramsbottom to send the car to take me home. He said he'd have it here by ten-thirty,' said Mrs Ramsbottom, getting up from the seat. She looks quickly into the basket. 'You didn't buy anything today Mrs Monro?'

'No. I didn't bring my purse Mrs Ramsbottom.' Mum starts to walk away.

'Put it on the books then! Mr Purdie won't mind. He lets all his reliable customers do it.' Mrs Ramsbottom smiles and her eyes go narrow. 'Unless of course...'

Mum and I walk on.

'Cow!' Mum says suddenly. 'She knew I couldn't buy anything! She had her ear hard against the shop doorway while we were talking. She'll tell all the neighbours.'

I try to pat her arm but she is walking very quickly, her shoulders and her mouth down. We get home and Mum dumps the basket in the kitchen.

'I wish I had some tea,' she says. I wish she had some as well. 'Don't worry,' she says to me. 'Tuesday's not far off and we can manage until then. You just go outside while it is fine, and play.' I give her a cuddle and leave but I'm still worried.

I go to the hut in the middle of the bamboo and sit on the old box I have for a seat. I look in the treasure box: there is only a dead weta with one of the back legs off, some string and one golden earring Mum gave me. Then I remember the rubies. The tin is nearly full of them, well nearly, and I sit down again and run them between my fingers. Most of them are much bigger than Mrs Ramsbottom's ones. Not as shiny, but bigger.

I think about Mrs Ramsbottom—about what she said and about her jewels and about how her mouth looks and about her b-t-m. Then I know what to do.

I walk out of our place to Mrs Ramsbottom's front fence. It is white with new paint. The lawn is just mown and I can smell the grass. The house is tidy-looking as well. The dark brown blinds are pulled down almost to the bottom of the windows. They all line up neatly. One at a time I throw the rubies hard onto her lawn, onto her path, onto her verandah. But soon I am throwing them up in the air and all over the place. I laugh. Rubies bounce in the grass and shine among the stones of her path. I throw them all. Then I throw the rusty baked bean can onto her verandah and run away fast before she can see who did it.

Crimson Poppies

Karangahape Road is a cat on heat I reckon. Has been for years. Well, that's what I thought that night when I went outside for a smoke and a look at the crowds. Yeah, a cat on heat... Toms are attracted from miles around for cash-and-quickie sex. Prowling. You can just about put them into boxes: businessmen, scurrying and looking around before scuttling into the "Scarlet Lady" or some such place; stag-party bridegrooms with their mates, drunk and egging each other on; the ugly randy ones desperate for sex; the gay men... Yes, you get to know the Toms....

Of course you get to know the girls and some of the boys too — I see them most on a Friday or Saturday night when I keep the Palm Café open till late. Quite a few of them come in for a cup of coffee to set them on their backs again, if you'll pardon the expression. There're the young ones trying it out because they've had fights with their Mums and the old ones on the game hoping to get enough for the kids or the drugs. The high-flyers with flashy cars and flash rooms—and the ones who'll do a knee-trembler down an alley for cheap. Lickerish-all-sorts I always say.

K Road's been like that for years. Well, this last twenty anyway: That's how long it is since Frenchie and me came to Auckland and bought the café. I reckon it'll still be the same in twenty years more too, even though they're always trying to clean it up—take down all the signs with naked ladies and such. After all, it's human nature, isn't it, to want—well you know what I mean. Like I always say, all of us want loving in one way or another... Take the couple that came the same night, about eighteen months ago (near as I can guess). They stood out in K Rd like a couple of crimson poppies in a wheat-field. I wondered what on earth they were doing there till I remembered the Hearts and Flowers dating place just opposite. They must've arranged to meet there and both of them wore great white-carnation buttonholes. Not that they needed the flowers to be noticeable.

It was only about eight in the evening on a Saturday, but the regulars of the street were already about. I remember the noise of some footie fans drowning their sorrows or celebrating their win at the Naval and Family. A drunk who'd turned up almost every darned day for the past five years wobbled along the footpath then stopped to throw up in the gutter. Disgusting. A couple of the working girls stared at the carnationed couple, sniggered and walked on.

Well, the pair with the buttonholes looked uncomfortable. They peeped sharpish at one another then looked quickly away again and her hand half hid her carnation like she wasn't sure whether to show it to him or not. He was about forty-something I guess—and not rolling in money judging by the somewhat old-fashioned suit and heavily creased shoes he wore. His face was tanned and good-looking, with dark blue eyes trimmed with beaut long eyelashes. A girl'd love those! She was no beauty, but nice enough. Wore a floral frock and carried a white plastic handbag with a gold clip. I like a good leather handbag, myself.

Kiwi women don't shake hands much do they? So I

watched him shove his hand out and her start to stick hers out just as he took his back again—all out of kilter. Finally she just put her hands behind her back as they introduced themselves. They obviously had nothing planned beyond the meeting—and soon their heads were looking up and down the road in time—like people at a tennis match. Well, I knew they'd head for my place—it was the only coffee place open and they didn't look the types to get stuck into the hard stuff.

He held her elbow as they made their way through the traffic. Nice that, and you don't often see it now do you? I didn't want them to see me rubbernecking so I scuttled back inside before they got over and stubbed my cigarette out in the sink. Can't really remember what they ate—but I bet it was a date scone for her and an iced bun for him since they had that every other time they came in. And a pot of tea of course. Always the same thing—except that every other time they came it was early in the afternoon. Course I came to realise it was the bus timetables caused that.

Gawd, I rabbit on eh? That's what Frenchie, my husband, used to say: "If ya couldn't open ya mouth the bloody words'd choke ya." But he always laughed and gave me a quick squeeze when he said it, bless his heart.

Now, at this point I have to say I'm an eavesdropper. I'm not ashamed of it. Do it all the time. Like I always say, it's not like opening other people's letters. I'd never do that. It'd be wrong to use what I hear for blackmail too—but I'd never do that either. I just get bored at slack times in the coffee shop and my feet ache and it takes my mind off them—and I'm a romantic—and want to know my 'regulars' anyway.

I do it by sort of tricking people into sitting at a certain table, and these two did it every time. Yes! To start with, I don't set to and clean up all the tables right away when the place slows down after about two o'clock on shop days. I don't mean I leave them all mucky: I mop up all the dribbles and crumbs with a cloth and just leave the odd cup and saucer and so on lying about. Now—the one I want folks to sit at—that one's cleaned up a treat and I always make sure there's a nice bunch of marigolds or something on it. It looks nice and private in the corner and they nearly always sit there. Too right! But the dodge is that the mirror on the wall there is actually a one-way window, and the wall's so thin that by pushing my ear on it I hear pretty well every word. When Mr Thompson sold Frenchie and me the Palm Café, he said we could keep an eye out for shoplifters through the window, and I do now and then when I remember... but really, any poor beggar who needs to pinch a doughnut or something... Well, anyway, by the time I'd made myself a cup of tea and could sit down behind the wall to listen, they'd already done the introductions and were trying to get to know one another. It turned out his name was John and hers was Maryanne.

'Yes,' he was saying, and he leaned back in the chair and laced his fingers behind his head. 'I've got this farm: dairy. Pedigreed Jersey cattle. Best land in the country, the Waikato! Best butterfat records. Only problem is now there's all this talk about butter not being good for the old ticker. Silly talk—but my word—it's affected sales since they've let margarine be sold in New Zealand...' He shook his head. 'It's not natural. It's idiotic—against our own interests. I mean if the farmer's not making money, no one in New Zealand'll make money. Backbone of the country—yes—backbone of the country.' John leaned forward and drank some tea. 'Now, that's enough about me for now. What about you?'

'Well, I'm separated and I've got two kiddies.' Maryanne spoke softly. I really had to push my ear to the wall to hear her. 'I'm working as a packer in a shoe factory—tennis shoes. I actually trained as a bookkeeper but it's not easy getting work that fits in with the kids' school hours so I suppose I'm lucky. Do you have any children?'

'No. Never married. Too busy. My mother lives with

me. She looks after me pretty well—good cook. Knows how to cook a roast just how I like it. Of course I run the odd Angus for beef and butcher a beast as we need it. I pack it for the deep freeze. So I'm a packer too! I shouldn't like you to think I'm totally useless around the house! We eat well—export quality. Mind you I sell off the better cuts. No sense in not making some money from the animal...'

So he went on. Boring I'd call him—but they got on real good. He could only meet her every second week as that was when Maryanne's ex had the kids and anyway it wasn't easy getting away from a town-supply dairy farm. Apart from his nice looks, I really couldn't figure out what Maryanne saw in him. He didn't have much money on him as far as I could tell by peeking in his wallet when he opened it. He even seemed reluctant to pay for the tea and stuff, and that didn't cost much. Bit of a tightwad I thought: there was a definite slowness of his hand as it got near his wallet pocket. I came to wonder if the story about all those cows was true. I mean, surely he'd run to a car and a few flash clothes if he owned a farm, wouldn't he?

But Maryanne liked him all right. She started wearing a bit of make-up and perfume and lost a kilo or two. And she always leaned forward and put her head on one side when he talked, you know, a bit like a blackbird when it's about to catch a worm. Even when he rambled on about the calves getting bloody scours or something— and I thought that was downright disgusting, she listened as if he was proposing marriage.

I worried about how it was going. Months went by and nothing seemed to happen. Just the tea and the cakes and the chat for an hour or so before he had to get the bus back home. Mostly he talked about the farm and mostly she talked about her kids and the people she worked with at the factory. Maryanne began to forget the make-up and a bit of a resigned look came into her face. I didn't blame her—it was so humdrum!

Then one day, things were different. It makes me

mad... Y'see, at the very time the thing started I had to serve another customer. I didn't mind right then—thought Maryanne and John would just have another boring and aimless chat. I was beginning to wonder how I could keep them out of my listening table.

But when I took my aching feet out of the flat shoes I always wore and settled down with a cuppa, I was onto a good exciting eavesdrop. Great! I could hardly believe it was John talking! I wished Frenchie was still with me. He would've loved it. Mind you, he'd probably have laughed out loud and spoiled the whole thing.

'Men are different,' John was saying. 'They have needs—drives. I feel I can talk to you frankly—we've known each other for quite a time now. When a man wants—well—you know—nooky—he'll crawl over an acre of broken glass to get it! The urge is that strong and overpowering. I wonder if you can understand that Maryanne.' Maryanne nodded vigorously.

'There's an ache in a young man's loins. His body must have release. He can think of nothing other than sex! There can be no higher goal—no other achievement unless that need is met. I'm convinced it's a natural hunger—just like being starving for food: As natural as the rutting stag or the bull that finds a cow on heat. It just takes over and must happen. You see?' He ran his fingers rapidly through his hair.

Whew! I shot a quick look at Maryanne to see how she was taking it. She'd turned all pink and was leaning forward so far she was nearly on the table-top. Her mouth was hanging open and her breath came quickly. Her eyes were dark and shone with delight. Her hands were more than halfway to his. She looked really pretty.

Well, John didn't stop there: He went on and on about the helplessness of a man 'compelled' as he put it, by sexual urges. Heavens, I was getting pretty pink myself! I was that pleased. After all, I'd been in on their first meeting and every one since. I knew what'd come next.

He'd make out something like he'd missed his last bus and could he stay at her place—or ask her down to the farm at Taupiri next weekend—or maybe he'd lash out and take her to a hotel room... but that seemed a bit unlikely. He might even propose marriage. I bet to myself that he'd have some good line worked out. Yes!

The darned "mirror" had steamed up but I wiped it silently with the dish-cloth and watched intently as John smiled, crinkling the corners of his nice eyes. He even touched her hand softly before saying with conviction: 'I'm so glad I'm past all that. A man's an absolute idiot in that state!' And he yawned. Yawned! And said something about how it was about time for his bus and they'd better be moving. I just couldn't look at Maryanne—but I knew she would've been as upset as I was.

They never came back to the Palm Café.

Head Hunting

'... We had our packs and guns to carry, enough grub for three or four days—as well as warm clothes: Bloody heavy. The 303's made it hard—they were army surplus and we'd cut the butts down to make them shorter and lighter, but even so, if we tied them to the packs they caught in the scrub and if we carried them we lost a hand grip.

'Me and Spence and Bert had gone into the bush behind Erua—quite near the old prison camp, down near Mount Ruapehu you know—and we had to clamber up an overgrown bush tramway. The timber was rotten and slimy and the second-growth manuka formed a tight tunnel we had to push through; hard enough to manage with two hands let alone one. By the time we got up near the tops, we were puffed out and filthy. The weather was starting to pack it in too.

'Didn't worry us though. Cripes, it was the first time we'd ever won a ballot for shooting in the forestry blocks and we were hoping to bag a sika, or, better yet, a red deer. This was well before the days when the helicopters whipped in and took all the game. Early seventies. You had a good show then of getting a head with some antlers for the wall and some meat for the family. Odds on. Deer were vermin rather than venison. We wouldn't carry out most of the beast; wouldn't even bother to gut it. Only carried out the best cuts and left the rest to rot. Same for pigs—not that I hunted them much. Best to have dogs for that, and Mabel drew the line at having hunting dogs at our place, eh Mabel.' I see Mabel nodding and knitting. I bet she hasn't heard a word I've said. John's listening though, so I carry on.

'We were a fair way up the slopes on a grassy area. First thing we did was get a fire going to boil water. Had a cuppa tea bush style—with a handful of manuka shoots in the brew. It's a corker drink that. But the clouds rolled in while we caught our breath, and the rain started. Just like that, eh.

'I mean, we thought we'd be Jake—after all, we were pretty well equipped. It was only a matter of minutes before we had Spence's tent up and nipped inside. Well, that was when we found out the old tent needed proofing. The water poured in—almost like the tent attracted the stuff! We gave Spence a right bawling out about that I can tell you! It was too late to pack it in and go home; the rain was bucketing down and we were buggered if we could see where the bush tramway was. Couldn't see past our fingers. So we decided to sit it out. I often wonder whether that was where we made our biggest mistake but, as they say, hindsight's twenty-twenty vision.

'There was no show of building up the fire again by then, but two of us had brought spirit burners and we brewed up something to eat. Rolled oats I think it was, because that was easy to cook and we followed it with chocolate and raisins and some good dollops of whisky. Things looked a lot brighter after that I can tell you!

'God, Dad, didn't anyone ever tell you about hypothermia and alcohol?' John looks amazed.

'No. Well, they might've—but we were well togged

out… anyhow we didn't have what ya call it?—hypothermia—did we.

'Now, to carry on: Spence had an oilskin cover for his sleeping bag, lucky bugger, but Bert and I didn't. We did the best we could by wrapping our parkas around our bags, but it was pretty useless. We all dressed in as many layers as we could and went to bed. I had my army trou and some good woollen long johns and that old blue sweater your Mum knitted when we were engaged. I threw that out last year because it had holes in it and Mum wouldn't darn it anymore. Anyway, I took a long time to drop off. I remember turning on my torch after an hour or two to look at the time and d'you know what?'

My son shakes his head. 'No,' he says.

'Bloody tent was full of stick insects—come on in to shelter I suppose. They'd've been disappointed! Jeez, it was wet! Y'could feel the cold creeping in with the water. But what with the whisky and the oats and so forth, I eventually dozed off for an hour or two… Bit uncomfortable but I had worse in the army. I was glad though when the sky started to lighten. I was stiff and cold and soaking wet and my skin was crinkled up all over. You know, like when your hands have been in water too long? Everything smelled sour and I've never been able to stomach the smell of wet wool since that night…

'The rain had stopped so I eased my way outside, lit up the burner and made a cuppa. Bert was still asleep and Spence was just beginning to stretch a bit. I picked up the cups to take into the tent…'

Something's… Something's bloody well… Crikey, my head hurts. My tongue won't work. It's filling my mouth… Can't even finish the… Mabel and John are staring; just waiting. Can't they see?

Mabel's dropped her knitting; wool rolling away… blue… blue… 'blue for a boy, Mr Wilson.' The Sister's holding John up to the nursery window for me to see. He's a bloody seal; round head and body tapering to nothing in all that shawl get-up. Poor little bugger can't move an inch. I desperately want to hold him; unwrap him and see he's all present and correct. Too bloody scared. Might drop him on his head. Not allowed anyway: Sister starched ramrod—no—might infect. Didn't expect to love him so soon… so much…

'It's all right Andy. The ambulance is on its way. Once we get you to the hospital they'll have you fixed in a jiffy.' Mabel is talking at me just like she talked at her Mum before she died: voice calm and reassuring but terror galloping about her eyes.

I'm going to die. I can hear, I can understand, but my mouth hangs open to speak and only spit flows out. My head has gone numb now but my body still lies skewed in the chair. There's an uncomfortable lump behind my shoulder blade—a spring poking up? I can't move. Stroke? How long? An hour or two? Weeks? I've had a good innings. I turned seventy-seven last month. But I don't want… too soon… always too soon… Haven't finished. Finishing's the important thing. I see my father yelling at me, face red and angry, *"The finish line's only ten yards off. Stop your bawling boy, and finish the race! You're acting like a girl!"* After I finished the race, blood squelching and sticky between my toes, father took me to have my knee stitched. I don't remember ever crying since… not once. Can't think clearly… what haven't I finished?

Not as if I can ask Mabel. She's talking to John now. His arm is around her shoulder. His stiff hand pats her arm—pat, pat, pat. Clockwork.

'He'll be all right Mum,' he says. Pat, pat, pat. 'Probably have to shoot the old bugger in the end. He's tough.'

Mabel laughs up as far as her eyes: 'You hear that Andy?' she shrieks, 'They'll have to shoot you John says! Shoot you!'

Not before I'm finished. Finished what though?

Finish the job? I've been a good provider… stayed in work all my life… The job was always unfinished. Sometimes John would call in at Prices' Foundry after school, hoping to walk home with me…*"I'll be home soon John, soon. Just tell Mum that Mr Pattison wants me to work a bit of overtime again…"* Never turn down overtime—you mightn't get another chance—the few quid I earned without penalty rates didn't go far enough with a growing boy. Six days a week making iron and brass castings. Hard men doing hard work but I worked my way up to foreman. John understood why I wasn't home much. He never wanted for anything. Always had new rugby boots. I used to have to play in bare feet… *"Stop bawling John, and get back in the game…"* Blood sticky on his face. Cut above the black eye. *"Don't be such a sook — get back in there now!"* Make a man of him. Make him a team man.

Somehow I'm in hospital. I must've conked out for a while but my head's clearer now. Must be the oxygen. Hate hospitals. Mabel and John are still with me. They're talking with a kid who reckons she's a brain doctor.

'This is Mr Wilson's MRI scan.' She points: 'Look at this difference between the left and right sides of the brain. See? There. The brain is compressed there—most probably blood escaping though there's a small possibility a tumour is causing it. When the theatre's ready we'll do an operation to relieve the pressure.'

'Will he live? Will he be able to speak again?' Good old Mabel's asking the questions I desperately want to ask.

'Well, Mrs Wilson at this stage it's difficult to predict the outcome. He's seriously ill. It depends upon two things: how much permanent damage has been done to the brain and what caused the compression. I mean, I've seen people recover from their speechlessness in a matter of hours once the pressure is relieved—but others don't ever recover. I'm sorry I can't be more specific. The anaesthetist will be along to talk with you shortly.' She dashes off, her long pigtail making her look even more childlike.

We wait for the operation. An anaesthetist talks with Mabel about my medical history: I can't even correct her when she says I'm not allergic to anything. She's forgotten how my hand swelled up with that bee-sting a couple of years ago. When he says he's going to do the operation with just a local anaesthetic I almost shit myself but apparently it's safer... Other doctors come in—a whole group along with the pigtailed doctor. After looking at all the machines I'm linked up to, and making a cheerful remark or two to John and Mabel, they settle into their jargon. At first I want to hear everything—but words like Broca's aphasia... embolism... infarct... don't mean much to me. I'm just a bloody rock sticking up in the river and the words flow about me. It's all in their hands.

I return to my own problem. What's niggling at me? Why is dying so bad right now? What haven't I done?

John's looking out the window. He tells me there's a harbour view out there. I stare at him. His face is tight and unhappy. His fingers drum on the windowsill. His wife chucked him out six weeks ago and he's been living with me and Mabel ever since. Is this my unfinished business?

I think about the last time they were at our place together. Evelyn was sitting as far away from John as possible. They were telling us they were getting separated and they started off calmly enough, but it wasn't long before they got angry. Evelyn said she'd had enough of John— didn't love him anymore. Said he didn't love her and never had. John's face had gone red and his fists clenched and unclenched on his lap. *"Rubbish,"* he'd shouted. *"It's not me wanting to break up the marriage! It's you."*

After he came back home I tried to get to the bottom of things. It was obviously not what John wanted. But all he'd say, with his lips thinned, was *"It's up to her. Not my choice. But if that's what she wants..."* and *"you know what women are like Dad..."* and *"if she wants to come crawling back it'll be too late..."* Yes. Somewhere in there is what's worrying me. Like a series of snapshots I see John and Evelyn together: at their wedding smiles into each other's faces and John making an awkward speech; when Michael was born, then Sarah. Things looked okay to me… but Mabel saw things differently.

More snapshots. Mabel saying to me: *"You're always too hard on John, Andy. He needs love, not criticism all the time"; "Why won't you talk with me?"; "Why can't you just say what you feel?"* Mabel's face isn't hard. It's sad. What does she think of me after all these years? Has our marriage made her unhappy? Does she even know how much I love her?

As sharply as a light house beam, I can see at last: John's just like me! He's useless at talking about soppy things… Useless.

The orderlies have arrived to take me to theatre but if I can ever talk again… As they wheel me away, Mabel kisses me and tears come to her eyes. John pats my shoulder, pat, pat, pat.

'Brace up Dad, you're a tough nut. You'll be okay.' His big hands drop to his sides; he clears his throat and turns away.

Today's the day when I try to put things right with John and Mabel. I got my voice back this morning. It's raspy and harsh, but I can speak. It's good-oh! The doctor with the pigtail warns me they may have to do another operation because apparently there's still bleeding going on and the drain in my head isn't right or something. She says I've got a long way to go before I'm out of the woods. She doesn't know the half of it. They'll be in to see me soon…

'I can chin wag again Mabel.'

Mabel smiles at me and her brown eyes sparkle. 'Well, that'll be the end of my getting a word in edgeways.'

'Yes. Well Mabel, well, it's good to see you… I've

something I want to tell you. Mabel... I... well... Where's John?'

'Just parking the car. He'll be up in a tick.' I look at the door. Sure enough, John's coming in.

'Here he is! Hello John! Come and sit down. I've something I want to say to you both.'

They sit and look at me expectantly. Nothing happens. Mabel's frowning.

'Are you all right Andy?'

'Yes. Give us a moment will you.' I look at them. My wife and my son. God, how I love them! It's driving me crackers trying to find the right words to tell them. I will though. Should have done it years ago. It's not sissy or weak. I'll tell John what he must do to get back with Evelyn and tell him how wrong I've been all these years. Just say it... My hands are flapping in the air and my face is wet with sweat. I know what I want to say. I just can't say it yet. Tomorrow. Tomorrow will be easier. I'll feel stronger then. I relax and try to cover the awkward silence.

'Remember that yarn I was telling you before all this happened? About Bert and Spence and me up Mount Ruapehu?'

They nod, looking puzzled.

'I didn't finish, did I? I will now. Where was I up to... That's right. I got back into the tent with the cups of tea and handed one to Spence. Then I went and shook Bert. He was dead.

'Just like that! Dead. Only thirty-six, with a wife and a kiddy. He was our best mate. I mean the night before he'd been joking and carrying on like usual... He was a real larrikin! I've no idea why he died. Could've been that hypo—what's it called? Hypotherm—what you said. I did always wonder whether the cold night finished him off. Or he could have had a dickey heart... Well, we tried to revive him but it was far too late. His face was all stiff.

'In the end we had to carry him out. We left him in his bag and started back down to the bush tramway. He was bloody heavy. We sort of dragged him along. It was all right while we were out in the open on the grass, but when we reached the tunnel of manuka we realised we wouldn't be able to manage. We couldn't find another way down. Spence and me sat down to catch our breath and have a think about it. I mean, we had to get him out somehow.'

I take a great shuddering breath to calm myself. I can see the two of us on the mountain with Bert's body.

'In the end there was no option. I took my hunting knife—the one I've still got, with the antler handle—and slit him open. I had to gut him to make him light enough for us to carry.

'Right inside, Bert was still warm and steam rose from the heart of him into the cold air. That made it worse somehow... Then we dug a shallow but lengthy hole with our bare hands and buried all his guts on the mountain… and we hauled the empty shell down.' Tears scald my eyes.

'Poor bugger never had a chance to say goodbye to anyone, let alone tell his family he loved them. He never said a word that night. Not one word.'

Sweet Charity

The school hall is hot and crowded. Diana's nose wrinkles—the guy with a grey beard and over-worn suit standing next to her stinks of old sweat. Perhaps that is appropriate. Redolent of adolescent smells... It couldn't be a coincidence that the word 'adolescent' encompasses 'scent'. Mind you, back in the fifties people didn't wash as often as they do now, so the school always ponged. Ponged? The slang and mean pinched post-war years of no soap, no flair and drab conforming rules, slips back into her head as though they own it. She shudders, eases away from the smell, and picks up a glass of wine. It tastes like tainted lolly water. She sips the sweet white wine and grimaces, wishing she knew enough about wine to say with authority: 'This wine has too much gobbledegook in it... Far too much...'

The hall is no longer used as a gymnasium—and all the varnished wooden ladders with thick dowel rungs and no grace, have gone. So are the webs of climbing ropes. Is it an improvement? Not noticeably. Her eyes flick to the board with Principals' names on it—yes, she could still see the lighter-coloured varnish where the heading of the board had been changed from 'Headmasters' to 'Principals'. The captains of the First Fifteens for the past umpteen years are listed in gold on a varnished board—so are the captains of the First Eleven and those ex-school males who made 'The Great Sacrifice'... and there in the corner another was a board with the captains of the girls' netball teams. She finds her name: Diana Cummings 1957. Line upon line of framed class portraits cover tired varnished walls and all carry their allotted patina of dust and fly-crap.

It was the first time she'd come back, but reunions were obviously popular: the hall hums and shrieks with ex-pupils searching for and finding their classmates. Diana couldn't recognise anyone. As she looks around, hampered by her lack of height, she knows who she is looking for: Miss Hopkinson, her second form teacher.

She no longer wants to kill her: but how she aches to flaunt her success. Diana looks at the multi-carat diamond flashing messages of financial security from her ring finger. She smiles as she thinks of the latest model Range Rover outside, the successful children she spawned, and the house in Paratai Drive with extensive views over the harbour. Smugly she smooths the skirt of the latest model she wears. She'll tell Miss Hopkinson all about her success, that'd show the old bat.

Amazing how the anger and humiliation remained fresh. It wasn't as though she'd focused on school at all once she'd left. She'd been too busy getting into business, marrying an equally ambitious man, and making money. Lots of money... involuntarily she imagines herself rubbing fistfuls and fistfuls of golden coins hard against Miss Hopkinson's face to force her to see her worth.

No sign of her so far. Andrea, who'd talked her into coming to the reunion, hasn't arrived either. Andrea had been Miss Hopkinson's pet, not a wholly comfortable thing to be—but far better than the alternative.

"Sit up Diana. Don't sprawl all over your desk like

some sort of serpent! Put your feet flat on the floor—Flat! Now put your exercise book so, and hold your pen thus, and write properly..." The times when she nagged were the best times: It was when she silently stalked the class she was most terrifying. She'd move around the room gently tapping a ruler onto her free hand. No one dared look to see where she was. They all sat cowed and mute, other than for the noise of scratching nibs or the sound of a pen dipping into the desk inkwell. Then she'd strike. A hand reached for a pigtail to yank an immature head back to stare into her unmoved eyes before she pushed the head forward onto the page.

"Look at that!" she'd hiss. "You've hardly completed any of the exercise, and *what* a grubby piece of work. Go to the front of the class and do your work like a baby—on the blackboard in chalk." No one would look at miscreants. Miss Hopkinson would grab and twist an ear to yank them to their feet and march them into shame at the front of the room where everyone could see them. They tried desperately not to cry. To cry brought more invective... and times without number she had seen Miss Hopkinson cut into the backs of hands with the edge of that ruler. Automatically, Diana looks at the back of her hand. She thinks she can still see a scar.

Should she have come back? It'd stirred up so many images she'd rather forget. Miss Hopkinson had left more than scars on the hand. Perhaps the worst was the time she saw Diana wearing a cheap metal ring... she had slapped the hand and confiscated the ring. That'd hardly mattered: it was the words that penetrated like acid.

"Did you steal that ring? Did you?" An ear was twisted.

"No, Miss Hopkinson."

"Where did you get it then?"

"In a Christmas cracker, Miss Hopkinson."

"Rubbish! You're lying! How could your mother afford Christmas crackers?"

"It's true Miss Hopkinson!"

"Well, more shame to you if it's true! Your family lives on the taxpayers of New Zealand. They wouldn't be pleased to see their money go on rubbish like Christmas crackers." To be accused of theft and then... Better to forget... A woman waves at her as she pushes through the crowd, but Diana has no idea who she is. Eyes gleaming, and with a wide smile she wends her way to her side.

'Diana! Diana Cummings! You haven't changed a bit! You look wonderful!'

Right. Diana attempts to look radiantly happy to see this stranger.

'You don't remember me do you? Ngaire! Ngaire Simpson! Well, actually I'm Ngaire Wood now.'

Instantly, Diana remembered. Ngaire had been the other charity girl in their class. 'You've changed so! Your hair!' Ngaire in her intermediate school years had mousey straight hair but now it flamed red and curly; sort of a hippie look.

They shouted short biographies at one another. Ngaire had four children, a husband named Jack, and a puppy called Murchison. She worked in the Work and Income Department, managing an office in South Auckland, and loved her job. Her husband was an entomologist researching some genus of weta named something sounding like 'net is' to Diana. Ngaire looked like a stereotyped earth mother, Diana thought. Her dress was flowing, floral and free over her soft plump body—and she glowed with health and happiness.

'Remember the uniform?' Diana had thought of the contrast.

'Couldn't forget that!' Ngaire laughed. 'The three pleats front and back tunic—remember ironing in those pleats? And the girdle I used to pull so tight to show I had a waist—and I did then! Miracle the thing didn't break or cut me in half!'

'Yeah! Stockings too—black lyle—at least when they

were new. They turned an awful greeny colour after a couple of washes didn't they.'

'Hmm. And do you remember how they had no stretch and yet it was social death to have them bagging at the knees so we hooked them up to our suspender belts so tight we could hardly sit down! Hey, and remember when the button came off the suspender belt we used to use a threepenny bit to hold the stocking up! Hurrah for pantyhose!'

'I'd forgotten that...' Diana smiled.

'Tell you what though—I got to try all sorts of new things at this school: remember the diving club? You were in that with me—and we got to try scuba diving at Waiheke Island with all the boys. I think we were the only girls in it, right? As for the music! The choir. Singing rotten gloomy hymns at assembly—"my heart was black with sin"—but singing pop songs in the playground at lunchtime. Remember the booklets we used to share with all the words of the songs in them? Learned to cook too— bloody useful when the kids arrived... I've good memories of my time here.'

Diana gasped. 'But what about the teachers? Downright sadistic! Surely you remember Miss Hopkinson?'

'Yeah—poor old thing wasn't she. I bet she hated teaching us as much as we hated her.'

'Oh, come-on Ngaire! No excuses! What about the ruler on our hands? And you must remember John wetting himself because he was so scared of her?'

'Sure. I remember. And I remember too, that my work improved like crazy in her class. I was too scared not to work hard! It was the times, wasn't it Diana. All the teachers used heaps more punishment than they do now. Totally unacceptable now—but just the way it was then—don't you think?'

'No! It isn't ever acceptable! I mean, do you remember how it was to be a charity kid here?'

Ngaire frowned. 'What d'you mean?'

'We were the only ones in our class living on a benefit. My Mum was a widow and got the Widow's Benefit. Miss Hopkinson never let me forget that did she! And she wasn't the only one. Even when we got our free stationery, they used to call our names out on the loudspeaker to come to the office and collect it. It was so demeaning. They couldn't have made it more obvious, could they?

'I used to walk up to the office window where Mrs Thompson handed the stationery to me. She'd act as though it was a gift from her own pocket. "Say thank-you," she'd insist. I hated it. I swore then I'd never let my kids grow up on state handouts and I've worked hard my entire life to make sure we had more than plenty — and lots in reserve. I always felt bitter that my Mum never went out to work.'

'Good grief, is that how you felt about it? I loved it! Thought I was the luckiest kid in the class. I'd march up to the office and Mrs Thompson gave me new pencils, new exercise books — even a new rubber! Then I'd go back to the classroom, absolutely sure I was better than the others who didn't get all that stuff for free... It was like prize giving! One of the memories that made me go and work for the Department — making sure other kids got a bit of a chance!'

Diana and Ngaire stared incredulously at one another. At last Diana said quietly, 'So what happened to Miss Hopkinson anyway?'

'Dead. Some pituitary trouble I heard.'

Dead. Diana shrugged and pushed quietly through the crowds with Ngaire. She'd get another glass of that sweet white wine, and then, maybe another. As she walked to the small kitchen hatch, now an overcrowded bar, she quietly turned the diamond to the inside of her finger.

Ash Wednesday

He is dead. The undertaker phoned me today to ask what I want to do with his ashes. He said they only keep them for three months… So he is dead—despite the dream.

There you lie in one of the coffins we saw in the ruins of Holyrood Abbey. You remember that abbey where the gargoyle heads wept onto eroded plinths? You know those coffins. Heavy, open, stone coffins shaped to hold the head steady and the body still: You lie there with a breeze ruffling your thinning hair— and you try ruefully to move your stone-restrained shoulders.

'This coffin doesn't fit too well—I must have gained weight,' you tell me.' I was so embarrassed—you shouldn't talk at your own funeral. But then I relented—laughed—and said, 'Get out of that and we'll go to that pub in Leith for dinner…'

But he is dead. And now I have this tiny box of ashes. I expected more: A large dark shiny grand-piano-wooden box with a silver plaque bearing his name. Not this—this white Queen Anne Chocolates cardboard box with a pale yellow label typed: Name, Date of cremation, and a number.

You didn't do it properly. Death that is. You were sup-

posed to demonstrate feelings of anger at your fate; then denial; and then and only then, acceptance. But as your skin yellowed and grew too large—sagged like ill-fitting panty-hose—you didn't share those feelings with me. You asked about others— and seemed interested in the answers. Yours became the emaciated ascetic face of a saint. I was the angry one. I wanted you to fight—to scream at the fates—to stay with me. But you died. And although you died right in my arms and I washed your body and put it into clean pyjamas and onto a clean bed and kissed the chill of your brow and put flowers in your hands—I don't believe you've gone.

I don't know what to do with these ashes. I DON'T KNOW WHAT TO DO WITH THESE ASHES. Is it legal to scatter them anywhere—like confetti at a bride?

Our granddaughter married last weekend. And you remember the brandy bowls we bought in a sale and never used? They were used at her wedding! A ceremony with a toast and a bit of poetry in it. You'd have loved all the fuss. She wasn't a flapper bride like me—but lovelier. And he didn't have your military stance—but he looks kind and in love.

They flew off somewhere for their honeymoon. More money than we had. We borrowed a bach—remember the shock when we discovered it only had a hammock? How we laughed as we pulled cushions and rugs down onto the floor for a bed. How much we enjoyed each other's bodies.

And then the Depression came and we had bought our rural retreat at the peak of land prices—just before the crash— rough land near Kawhia. I remember how you said you could write a list of hundreds of ways to use a kerosene tin: to boil up the sheets or the spuds—or cook the fresh fish right on the beach or heat the water for the bath… we even used one as a drum to celebrate the end of the War. You made it all seem a picnic… even when you had to make furniture from cheese boxes and crates and I had to make the children's panties from the soft white flour bags—with `Champion' written across their bottoms. You used to say how lucky we were to be in the country with a veggie garden and a few chooks and fat sheep. Luckier than the 'townies'.

I really thought you enjoyed it all—but knew better that day when you got stuck in the mud. You know—you were carrying Dorothy on one arm and a kerosene tin of scraps for the pigs on the other—and you sank in the mud up to the top of your gum-boots. You laughed at first but all of a sudden you yelled and swore and threw the tin down, frightening Dorothy... You screamed at the fates then... and eventually we won. The depression never quite left us though, did it. You always were so pleased when you bought socks—drawerfuls—and I still love lots of lacy, pretty frilly undies.

I don't really want to part with the ashes. It's all I've got left of him. I'm getting enough advice. I could get a military plaque for them. Or scatter them on Lake Taupo where our holidays were spent. I could endow a public garden with a tree and feed it with your ashes nestling underneath. But I don't really want to. I want to be allowed just this little bit of you. I'm told that's morbid—unhealthy...

If you could only hear the advice I'm getting. You'd laugh with me. Or cry. People's perceptions of me in the role of widow vary so much. I must get another man—or a companion (imagine that!). I should give away all your tools—should keep them. I should not make any decisions—should sell our house—should not sell our house—should join a club, should give myself time—should, should, should. You'd think that being bereaved equated to a frontal lobotomy.

I've come to think that there's a difference in how we expect women to grieve compared to men. 'For men must work and women must weep'—and I want to do both and so would you, wouldn't you.

I want to keep going: Remember what we said solemnly to each other the day they told us you were going to die very soon? We struggled to accept that and vowed that every day we had would be lived to the hilt. And mostly it worked. And mostly it works now for me. Not always. Some see my struggle—others don't...

You must be dead. There is nothing to help me manage—

*you're not here to love away my hurt or lift my incubus. There's
no concern or cuddles. Just nothing. Nothing.*

So—I've looked into the cardboard box numbered
7283/103. Inside is a paper bag—neatly folded over at
the top like a packet of sugar. Inside the bag is two and a
quarter pounds of gritty grey ash. All that's left.

I make a cup of coffee, carry our photograph album
to the window seat we shared so often, and sit still in the
pale sun of the winter's day.

The Fortunes of War

'They should put more cushioning on these seats. Look. I can put my whole fist behind my back.' Jim's bony fist, with knuckles swollen like a jacks set, proves the point. 'It's all right if you're young—your back can take it. But this is an ambulance for goodness sake! Should be comfortable.'

'Couldn't agree more. I've often thought that,' Dave, on the seat beside him, said. 'It's not as if we're getting hauled off the battlefield to be patched up in some scruffy field hospital. Mind you, it's good to get picked up from home like this. I can't drive any more—my ticker's wonky—and I live a full hour from the hospital.

'So you were a serviceman then?'

'Yep—WW2.'

'Where'd you serve?'

'Greece and Crete. The big success stories!' They both laughed.

'Me too. Lucky to get out with my arse intact! Lots of my mates didn't make it.' They fell silent, their faces hard, their eyes soft.

Jim sighed. 'I was evacuated from Greece and sent

straight off to Crete. Then I was wounded leaving Sfakia in the evacuation—end of May 1941—and thought that was the end of my War. Taken back home. But I got better and was sent back—to Italy for my sins. What about you?'

'Bit like you in some respects. I was with the 4th Field Regiment—got captured then escaped from Galatas prison camp before they sent me to the POW camps in Germany. Spent the best part of a year trying to get off Crete. I found another couple of Kiwis—and the locals helped us. I admired that—it was risky. Many of them were shot for less than they did for us. They helped us with food even though they were short themselves. We hid in gullies they showed us in the hills—had some near misses when Germans were hunting for escapers. But eventually we managed to leave Crete in a caique. Close call though: we drifted for days before getting picked up by the Brits. Had no food or water by then and one bloke'd gone off his rocker and jumped overboard! Drowned. We blamed the salt water he drank.'

Dave grabbed the seat arm as the ambulance turned a particularly tight corner then continued: 'I was pretty crook—lost a lot of weight and had a broken arm that hadn't been treated so they sent me home. That was that really. The arm's never been right since then.

'But it was a long time ago. Lifetime ago. Nice to find someone else still alive: we're a rare breed these days. So when you got back—how'd you get on here? Got a family?'

Jim shifted uncomfortably on the hard seat. 'I'm probably going to shock you—what did you say your name was?'

'Dave—Dave Hill.'

'Well Dave—I'm old and haven't got time to waffle around making things sound nice. So I'll tell it as I saw it—warts and all. I'm sick of all the politically correct bull-shit.' He looked intensely at Dave, who moved slightly away from him, wondering whether he was a bit shell shocked.

'I married and had two kids. I don't mind telling you though—it was a mistake. The kind some of us made in the War. While I was in New Zealand recovering I was told I was going to have to go back and fight in Europe. I believed—no—I knew I'd be killed there. No doubt at all in my mind about that. I couldn't possibly survive another battle or evacuation. So many of my mates had already died.

'Then I met a girl who took a shine to me. We hardly knew each other but she was keen as mustard about me and I wanted all the things blokes normally want: sex, kids, home of my own... You know. I wanted to do all that before they sent me off again. She was a looker too! But as soon as we tied the knot I knew I'd done the wrong thing.

'We had nothing in common—and it was servicemen she was as keen as mustard on. Not just me. I went back to War thinking "what the heck, I'll be dead any day anyhow". But I didn't die.

'When it was all over and I came home, and we had a son by then, I felt I had to stick with her and raise the family. We bought a farm in Raglan. She'd lost her looks, nagged all the time, flirted with any man who visited us—even took to the bottle. I stuck it out for thirty-five years. Shit—what a waste!

'Life's been better since we divorced. I live in a bivvy on the end of my son's house now. He didn't take sides and we get on good-oh. His missus feeds me good tucker and I potter about growing a few vegetables to help them along. Their kids are off their hands now but visit us often. It's pretty good really. You asked!

'Now it's my turn—what about you Dave? How's life treated you?'

Dave sat silent for a time then blurted, 'I never married.'

'You got the best of it then in my opinion!'

'No! I wanted to marry! Before I left New Zealand I met a wonderful girl and we fell in love. I'll never forget her: the soft wavy hair she wore sort of clipped back to hold it off her face… Her mouth was so gentle but I got to kiss it just once just before I shipped out. I could go on and on—she was shy and tiny and all I wanted to do was to marry her and protect her forever…

'I wrote to her whenever I could while I was overseas but only had a brief letter or two. Her parents would have stopped her keeping up the contact. They disapproved of me. Not good enough for her. They might have been right—but no one would have looked after her better than I would have done.

'And then I got home and went to her place and her Dad told me she'd married! I didn't believe it for a long time. He wouldn't tell me her married name or where she lived. It pretty much ruined my life. I've never seen her since and wonder what happened to her. New Zealand's not a big country but I've never come across her even though I was a sales rep and travelled all over the place. She was such a delicate looking girl I wonder if she survived long.

'I never took to another woman—though I've had good friends who are women. It just seemed as though lightning could never strike the same place in my heart again. From those days to this I've carried her memory in my mind. Sounds daft doesn't it Jim.'

'Not really. I could envy you that memory.'

'Here,' Dave scrabbled about in his pocket and drew out a battered wallet. 'I carry her photo with me still.' He pulled a well-worn black and white photograph out of the wallet and handed it to Jim. 'She's lovely isn't she.'

Jim stared at the image, his face twisting.

'I don't know how to say this, Dave—or even whether I should. That picture is of my wife.'

The two old men stared at one another as the ambulance pulled up at the hospital. The ambulance driver came to the door to assist them. Still silent, they solemnly shook hands, shook heads and walked unsteadily into the hospital.

Hortense's Final Journey

Elizabeth died only four months ago and I am alone with one of her best friends having dinner. Although I am 'a free man' it feels wrong—and right—to be here.

This café is a quirky place, surviving in one of those old buildings in Devonport. The rimu floors amble up-hill and down dale with the rotting piles. Some amateur painter has turned the walls into a garish pink-purple colour and done a bad job of it: There are paint splashes on the floor and the scotia mouldings. All the tables are of old heart rimu with a lovely grain to them—and on them greyish looking candles stuck into wine bottles are trying to create atmosphere. Great food though—or was last time I was here. All sorts of odd things like kangaroo and crocodile on the menu as well as a long wine list demanding the palate perk up and take notice.

But it feels wrong. Elizabeth fills my mind still: I nursed her for sixteen months as she weakened and succumbed to mesothelioma. She figured she got it by licking her finger to turn over dusty stocktaking invoices in the room where the asbestos was stored; just a holiday job during the university break, so many years ago. If she hadn't been a smoker then she might not have... but she was.

For eight of the months after she left the hospital still with a drain in her side to channel the fluids forming in her chest, knowing there was nothing that could save her, we travelled around New Zealand. I put my business into the hands of my close friend and assistant manager, Ray, and rushed about buying a campervan. It was summer and there weren't many available that we could afford, but I found an ancient Bedford van converted into a camper. We dubbed it Hortense, and left Takapuna. Hortense was an error of judgement.

There were places Elizabeth wanted to see just once more and we got to most of them—storing up memories: New Zealand's landscape became dotted with them. Hortense insinuated herself into many of them. Taupo—Elizabeth had the drain removed from her side and Hortense needed a new tyre. Taranaki—as remote as it was possible to be; we were picnicking on a beach near the lighthouse when Elizabeth's body rebelled against the antibiotics she needed and came out in a rash all over—and Hortense delayed our search for medical help by overheating and hissing angry steam from her rusty radiator.

And in the South Island the relationship continued. In Kurow—April by then and Autumn was creeping onto the land with frosts and fine days—we were stranded when Hortense needed new parts to be brought from Christchurch. Elizabeth and I walked alongside the Waitaki River, marvelling at the juxtaposition of blue river and yellow autumnal trees immediately adjacent to the town tip, scattered with rotting sheep carcases. There was, thank goodness, a second hand bookshop in Kurow. In three days we knew the place overly well.

It wasn't only Hortense we had to overcome. Elizabeth wanted to—I don't know, she was in total denial for months—pretend that there was no death penalty.

I pretended too. It was if she knew reality but wanted to fight the disease off by making her body do all the things it did normally. And at the same time, she was scared of what might happen if she pushed too hard. My stomach churned as I imagined her hurting herself but I still wanted her to fly against the disease and live triumphantly, until she could no longer do so. Not to crumple, defeated, and wait to die.

So when she said wistfully she wished she could climb to the Okarito trig station—far above the lagoon where we were sitting to watch for kotuku—I wanted her to get there. A kotuku flew near us, its shining white feathers defined by the blue sky. The Māori whakatauki "He kotuku rerenga tahi", meaning it was a bird to be seen only once in a lifetime, decided me.

'We can do it,' I said, hoping I sounded confident. 'If you aren't fit right now, we will just take more time.' I surreptitiously put the emergency kit of morphine into my pocket. Her bones could be softening with the disease and could crumple if she fell. My heart thumped wildly even before we reached the slope. We started and stopped and stared into the bush for a time, then started again, inching our way up to the trig. Slowly. Slowly. But she won!

I have a photo of her by the trig—Mount Cook clear of clouds in the background. She's holding her thin arms above her head and smiling with her whole face…

As the months passed, I grew to be an old, old man, carefully choosing how we'd tread, pacing my walking to her breathing. Clasping her hand to my arm. Watching. Scared. Hoping I'd know enough to keep her safe and pain free. It was worth it though just to see her on a beach idly filtering the sand between her fingers or crushing manuka leaves to put in a billy full of tea I'd made on an open fire.

And those were the best months—months of beautiful sunsets and sunrises. Weeks of the smell of the bush and the heat of the sun on our bodies and enough health to make her laugh and believe she might win over the cancer. Months of loving carefully. She wrote postcards to the hospital ward showing place after place we'd been to—defiantly saying, "I'm still alive and kicking!"

Our voyage ended in Kaitaia. By stopping frequently and resting, I had nursed Elizabeth and Hortense around the East Cape and into Northland, following the last of the warmth. Hortense grew a leak which rained onto our feet as we slept, and her radiator also wept rusty water. On a steep hill south of Kaitaia, Hortense dropped her wheel assembly onto the road. I couldn't steer her, though god knows I tried, and she gouged a track across the road and into a ditch. Elizabeth, though terrified, was not hurt. I walked away from them both as nearby farmers talked to Elizabeth, and sobbed my terror and sorrow. Hortense was dragged to the wrecker's yard. It was time to go home.

Elizabeth's last months were home with me. Our home turned into a hospital: a hospital bed provided to help me move her; a bedpan then a catheter; thermometers, morphine, rejected meals of miniscule proportions; potions to massage into her now skeletal body to stop bed sores and masses of pillows to cushion her frailty; stainless steel bowls for vomit; large cotton buds and mouthwash to freshen her mouth; arms to cuddle her with and tissues to dry the tears. And love: a love so strong I almost came to believe my will would keep her alive. I lay on a mattress beside the bed and listened to her breath rasp and her arms flail. Sleeping became pretty impossible: I'd find myself involuntarily leaping from the bed, heart pounding, to check that Elizabeth was all right; time after time and night after night.

When she died, it was sudden. Her breathing changed and her skin turned grey. We had time only to squeeze hands—and she had gone. She was still in my arms—still warm when the ambulance arrived.

"She's dead," the ambulance driver said softly.

"I know," I replied.

Although visitors had come to see her and District Nurses aided in the last stages of her life with things like baths and shampooing her hair, most of the time she was ill she and I were alone.

On the day after her death I went to have a cup of coffee at the local mall. The noise and relentless stream of people drove me home again. An empty exhausted shell, I felt nothing other than in some strange way it was me who had died. For weeks after her funeral, I still leapt from the bed, panicking, to check that she was all right. I'd slowly return to remembrance and bed, only to have it happen again and again.

I had fourteen months where I knew Elizabeth was going to die and when it happened I thought I was coping okay considering. Oddly, though, the story of my loss shows up most clearly to me in the cheque butts I wrote at the time. My writing had shrunk and shaken to illegibility; recipients' names were absent, or dates, or amounts. Gradually they improved.

And now I am in the restaurant with Brittany. It feels right because I know her well and like her. I'd rationalised the dinner with her by saying things to myself like, "It'll just be a nice catch up chat and that'll be that. Nothing more."

But it isn't. As the pinot noir goes steadily down in the bottle, vino veritas kicks in. I find myself leaning further and further onto the table towards Brittany—and notice she is doing the same. I can smell her scent and like a feral animal I feel like howling at the moon with desire. The candlelight that polishes her chestnut hair and gilds her skin also reveals the huge pupils of her eyes.

Our conversation remained unmemorable but our intentions changed. And that became the night I knew for certain I was still alive.

Waiting for Brad

'He's gorgeous…' I accidentally say it out loud. The old cow sitting next to me looks pissed off. Like, what would she do if she was meeting Brad? I laugh. She's totally past it.

He said he'd meet me here at eight. It's only half-past seven, but I sweat like crazy if I hurry so I came early. This is such a cool café: I hope Jennifer sees me here…

'Yeah, Brad and I come here all the time. It's like, all right.'
I shrug. 'We enjoy the latté.' I take Brad's arm and smile up at him and flutter my eyelashes, like that article in 'Girlfriend'.
'Have you done it?' she asks. She wants to do it before me.
I pretend not to understand. 'What do you mean?'
'You know. IT. Have you done IT yet?'
I smile mysteriously. 'Well, what do you think?'
'Wow!"…

Jennifer's beautiful. Her Mum lets her have anything she wants. Like, this week she's got the shortest black skirt—it hardly covers her undies—and a top that looks like a black leather bra. My Mum says they'll be so out of fashion next year—and only let me get a pair of blue jeans and a white T-shirt. So lame!

My legs are itching. It's these tights I got to go with my red skirt. I knew I should get mediums, but Jennifer was with me so I bought the small ones. Twenty-five minutes to eight. I'll go to the toilet and…

Now what will I do? I've torn a hole in the fucking tights and my thigh has pushed through it like some disgusting cauliflower. Like, there's no blood getting through—I could get gangrene…

'Look Brad! Carol's got disgusting gangrene from having fat thighs! Mine look better don't they?' Jennifer shows Brad her thin brown thighs. While I'm dying of gangrene! They walk away holding hands… '

Twenty minutes to eight. I wonder if I should buy a drink. That's the third time that woman's wiped down the table and glared at me.

'I'm waiting for someone.' Not just anyone. Brad. What if he doesn't turn up? I'll die. He's like totally awesome. His eyes are clear blue like that actor in 'Home and Away'. I wish mine were like that.

I run my tongue over my teeth. I can feel something. What if it's a bit of my Moro bar sticking there? I rush back to the mirror in the toilets and with my finger rub my teeth like crazy. They look great: white and even. I've eaten all my lipstick so I put more on. 'Mmm,' I pout at the mirror and practice making my eyes sexy like. 'Wow,' I drawl at the mirror, 'I'm like so totally duh!' My voice is all echoey in here. A woman comes out of a cubicle and laughs at me as she leaves. I could die! I can't walk out there now! She'll be telling everybody about the moron she saw in the loo. Everyone'll be watching. I go back to the mirror.

There's a spot the size of an Egyptian pyramid on my chin! How come I didn't see that before? I squeeze it and all this disgusting pus flies out. Blech! I get some toilet paper and wipe it up. Now it's bleeding. Shit! I stick a small piece of the paper on the blood and wait for it to stop. I lean against the wall. Quarter to eight. What if Brad is early and I'm stuck in here?

I've got to get out. I'll pull my hair forward so no one will know it's me. I'll walk right back in there past that woman and find Brad... I peer around the door, ready to duck back in if the woman is looking but she's gone. There's no sign of Brad either. I remember to take the paper off my chin before I walk out. Phew. I keep my head down in case the woman told someone about me, and walk back to the table.

Some prick's sitting there! I glare at him. It's so unfair! I mean, I chose that table first. Right in the corner. Intimate...

'Carol.' His hand closes over mine and he stares into my eyes. 'Honey-babe! I've got tickets for us to see R.E.M. in Barcelona. I feel so lucky to be with you.'

'Yes, Brad, yes,' I agree...

The prick at the table says 'What the hell's your problem?' and I walk to an empty table in the middle of the café. Not nearly as nice. In the middle of the café: where everybody walks by and stares. Everybody can see I'm here on my own. I should've bought a drink. Then I'd look less conspicuous.

I sit down and hold my legs together tight, so the hole won't show. Then I put my elbows on the table and rest my chin gently on the tips of my fingers so I look deep in thought. I wish I hadn't got here so early. I wish I hadn't said I'd meet Brad here. I can't cry. I go all red and blotchy. Not like Jennifer. She cries and it's like, the tears come out but that's all: no blotches or noise or goo pouring out her nose...

'Brad, it's no good. We can't go on deceiving her this way,' tears pour down Jennifer's cheeks. She looks beautiful. 'We've got to stop seeing each other.'

Brad is crying too. 'No Jennifer! No! I love you!' Just like in mum's Mills and Boons...

Ten minutes to go. Should I leave now? Like, dump him before he can dump me?

'You on your own?' I look up. A man is standing smiling at me. He's wearing a suit and a red tie and carrying a mini iPod. I mean that's just so cool. He must be at least twenty. Mature. What should I say? I smile. I mean, if Brad walks in and I'm here with this man!

'At the moment,' I say.

'Well, would you mind if we sit here? The place is getting crowded.'

We? What we? He sits down and so does his girlfriend. She'd been behind him, carrying their cups of coffee. She's got long shiny hair like Jennifer's. He lights cigarettes for them both and they start to talk to each other, ignoring me completely. I mean, is that rude or what?

'Yoo-hoo, I'm here! Not part of the furniture. It's MY lungs you're filling with smoke and this is MY table. I had it first you know,' I think of saying out loud.

As if she heard me, the girlfriend decides to be sociable: 'And what school do you go to?'

'School?' I laugh derisively. But can they tell I'm still at school? I rush back to the toilet. My lipstick must have gone again. It has, and the mascara I pinched from my sister is in black streaks under my eyes where I rubbed them to get rid of the smoke itch. I look disgusting.

It's five minutes to eight. I must clean up somehow. I splash water on my face but the mascara sticks to my skin. Pity it didn't stick to my eyelashes like that. I get some liquid soap from the dispenser and apply that. It gets into my eyes and reddens them, but the mascara has almost gone.

I look once more into the mirror: Oh Yay! My skin and eyes are red and the pimple on my chin is starting to bleed again. I haven't dared bring my sister's makeup with me so the lipstick is all I have. A ladder has descended from the hole in my tights and I'm sure it's widening as I watch.

Why didn't my Mum let me do that course that Jennifer did? She learned makeup and clothing and ev-

erything... Jennifer and Brad are laughing at me.

'Look at her face! How could she go out with an enormous zit like that?'

'Looks as though she's washed her face with a pot-clean-er!' They fall about with laughter.

'And the hole in her tights!'

'And a ladder firemen could climb!'

'What a fuckwit!' They turn and kiss each other: a long kiss with their mouths open. Brad puts his tongue inside Jennifer's mouth. It's disgusting... I leave the toilet. Brad is there, walking up to me. He smiles briefly then closes his mouth like a trap and looks worried. Hah! I saw though! He's got new totally disgusting braces! Blech! Brad looks at me, trying to smile with his mouth shut...

Brad is kissing me. The braces cut his lip and he bleeds and tries to mop up the blood with a paper serviette.

'It wasn't meant to be this way Carol!' Tears spill out of his beautiful blue eyes.

He is still like totally gorgeous...

'Hi Brad,' I say, smiling widely. I remember to flut-ter my eyelashes and touch his arm.

The Glorious Dead

"The Glorious Dead" the cenotaph says—rain and harsh lights polish the words. The ANZAC flags cling to their standards and Sam can see most of the crowd isn't sure whether they should put up their umbrellas or not. Most don't, and rain pounds their heads. There's more than the usual number of service personnel, chaplains, and civvies today. Sam sits silently in his wheelchair, head uncovered and water wending its way inside his raincoat.

The welcoming speech, by some army bloke who probably never left his desk, is stuck back in Gallipoli: "casualties on our side were 33,000 killed, 78,000 wounded and 8,000 missing..."

'How many died in our War, eh Ernie?' Sam mutters to himself.

A hymn starts, and he sings in his quavering voice along with the straggle of singers who don't know the words and probably cannot read their wet hymn sheets. "Abide with me: fast falls the eventide..." Too right. He can feel the roughness of his ridged fingernails and the crispness of his skin even in the rain. His thighs are so thin his arthritic knee joints bulge. He sighs.

He's supposed to stand now for the prayer, and it hurts that he can't. Eternal Lord God we pray for the peace of the world..." Not me, he thinks. His prayer would slaughter the Japs, for starters. Those bastards deserved the atom bomb—deserved more of them in fact. But just a few years after the War everybody bought Jap crap and set up sister cities and what have you. Now you've got these soppy peace and love types—they weren't even born when the War was on.

He liked the prayers they said at Dawn Services years ago. They weren't about peace: "We bless you for the dauntless courage of those defenders of our country who have fallen in the cause of truth and righteousness..." That was more like it. God was on his side then.

The wreaths are laid. He watches red poppies bloom with laurel leaves against the granite cenotaph. Some people bend stiffly from the hip and plant their offerings firmly so the wind won't move them. Others have done it many times before; they place their wreath briskly then whip off a snappy salute and back off the cenotaph to their places. Wreaths pile up from the RSA, the Army, Navy and Air Force: Wreaths from the Fire Service, the Police, the Girl Guides and Scouts, and—good Lord—the Hiroshima Commemoration Committee.

Sam shakes his head and takes his thick glasses off for a good wipe with his white handkerchief. Everybody else stands again. The pure notes of the "Last Post" un-man him and a tear merges with the rain. Time for one minute's silence now.

'Oh, Ernie, what would you make of it all?'

Every Anzac Day is the same, throwing Sam back into his second year of captivity, a prisoner of war on the Thai-Burma Railroad: He doesn't know the date, but probably 1944, monsoon season.

'Hey! Tenko in a minute. You'd better get up!' Ernie

was right, but although Sam managed to sit up and push his legs off the bamboo sleeping platform, he was too dizzy to move. Rain pelted the thatching of the hut and dripped onto them.

His leg stunk and he peered at the ulcer on his shin. It'd grown larger—about four inches long now—bloody bamboo—just a nick in the skin and the tropical ulcers started. The crater of his ulcer under the thin scab brimmed with pus, and when he wiped it with his finger he found his shinbone exposed and suddenly felt crook. One of those biting bugs appeared beside him but when he grabbed for it, it slid between the bamboo slats and disappeared. He almost fell, so lay back again. What had Ernie said just then?

'If you can get down to the river and stick your leg in, the fish'd eat off the dead flesh. John did, and it worked. Mind you, he had salt to pack in it as well. Dried it up.' There was no medicine—just one package of Epsom Salts for the camp of hundreds of men.

'I can't work today.'

Ernie frowned. Sam knew the look; almost heard the whirring of Ernie's brain. They'd been friends since they were kids in Masterton, but Ernie was the bright one who went to uni then came back to teach social studies at their school. Sam stayed home on the family farm until the war. Thank goodness they'd managed to stay together so far.

Sam grinned. 'Y'know, Ernie, with that sour look on your face, and the fundoshi nearly falling off your bum and all, you look like the world's skinniest sumo wrestler! Lightest flyweight ever!' Like most of them, Ernie's bones pushed at his dirty skin. Those glands, what did Ernie call them? Lymphatic, that's right. They never knew they had them before but after months of starvation they stuck out like dog's balls.

'Oh hell Sam, be serious. Pigface is on duty today.' Pigface was the Jap gunso who supervised the count of them at tenko; real name Watanabe. He regularly strutted about the camp with a sword at his side and a rifle over his shoulder, looking for trouble. 'You sure you can't manage one more day if I help you? Tomorrow's a yasumi day, so you could rest up then.'

Sam had seen Watanabe poking the tip of his sword into the gut of a prisoner who said he was unfit to work. The poor bugger had leapt from the pain and was told he was obviously fit to work... Sam tried again, managed to stand upright, and put his fundoshi and hat on. He hadn't had shoes for about a year, but his feet had toughened up good-oh. It was okay unless the latrines overflowed...

Ernie held his arm at the elbow and half carried him outside to the line-up. 'Least we're getting washed,' Ernie muttered as the rain intensified. 'Least it's warm.'

Pigface was late, and when he did arrive, he glared at them. The guards with him carried bamboo poles ready to strike out any protest. There was a speech before the count:

'Obedient to the Imperial Command issued by His Majesty the Emperor, I shall require all of you to work harder since nobody is permitted to do nothing and yet eat. Speed-o is our watchword.

'The hand of the Nippon Army Railway Construction Corps is to hurry and connect Thailand and Burma. The work must be finished by August...'

Pigface and the interpreter eventually stopped and the count began.

'Ichi, ni, san, shi...' the prisoners counted themselves along the line. The Nips let them do it: they never got it right. Sam swayed and fell. As he rose to his hands and knees, a guard hit him across the shoulders and he slumped face first in the mud. Pigface booted him in the ribs.

He heard Ernie shout, 'He's sick! You stupid bastards! Can't you see he's sick?' Ernie grabbed Pigface's arm.

Sam scrabbled to his feet.

'I'm standing! Look! I'm standing!' Sam shouted as Pigface signalled the guards to use the bamboo rods on Ernie. Pigface screamed his anger. As the blows hammered Ernie to his knees, Pigface held the barrel of his rifle and repeatedly whacked the butt into Ernie's skull. He fell, unconscious.

There was a roar from the prisoners, and Pigface pointed his rifle at them. The prisoners, unarmed, fists clenched, stared him down but could do no more.

Sam kneeled next to Ernie. Silence. Pigface and his guards retreated a few yards.

'Ernie?' Sam lifted Ernie's head. It was split, and his clever brain slid in blood covered lumps to the ground...

A week later, Sam had his leg removed: gangrene from his ulcer. Of more than two hundred amputations in the camp only thirteen lived, so he was lucky to survive. But the amputation was messed up and at his hip, so he couldn't have a prosthesis fitted. Used crutches until he got old and weak...

He's missed the Reveille now. A chaplain, probably Catholic looking at the frock thing he's wearing, is having his say. The heads of the crowd are bowed — is it a prayer? Sam wonders what it would be like being a Catholic. Would confession and a penance have scrubbed out the guilt he felt about Ernie?

Automatically he glances at his watch; nearly over for another year. Usually about this time he thinks about the beer or two he'll drink with his mates to drown his sorrows and have a catch up. This year though, for the first time, a memory of Ernie young and alive in the camp slid into his head.

Ernie, Sam and some of the others sat outside their huts. It was one of the rare yasumi days and the locals came in with small amounts of food to sell. They bought duck eggs with the miniscule amount of money they earned on the railroad, and added them to the usual small and dusty rice serving along with a bit of green stuff they picked from the riverbank. The brew smelled good. Luxury.

Talk between them was pretty well used up: they'd sung songs, related their early childhood stories, described the wife and kids and told yarns about life on civvie Street. They'd talked about all the camps they'd been in and rumours about new camps they would be sent to—and gossiped about the Japs; the better ones and the worse.

But, on that day, one of the Aussies talked about the end of the War for some reason. Maybe, thought Sam, maybe he knew something, had heard something. Maybe he was getting the griff on a hidden radio. He talked as though the end of the War was close... It wasn't something Sam usually thought about. It was enough just to get through the day. Try and keep the shit off your feet. Kill a few bugs by running a flame under your sleeping platform. Carry enough loads of dirt or rock for the rail. Eat every grain of rice and anything else you could pinch. Poke your finger into your swollen ankles to see how far the beriberi had progressed... He joined in. 'I hope they line up all these Nips and shoot them.' Some of the others nodded.

'We're going to have to live with them somehow.' Ernie spoke slowly. He stopped to roll a skinny smoke with a page from his Bible. Up to the last of the Psalms now, Sam noticed. Best paper for fags. Thin. 'They probably need to resurrect the League of Nations or something. I even wonder whether Germany would've got stuck in this time if the Great War surrender terms weren't so harsh. You've got to remember the world's getting smaller—what with aeroplanes that'll be used for travel and trade once the War ends. So we'll have to move on... learn to make peace with each other.' He sucked on the cigarette then said, 'Y'know, not everything our guys have done is squeaky clean either...'

Sam shakes his head. Rain released from his hair drops onto his chest full of medals. Move on! Just forget the thousands of deaths on the railroad alone! Almost a quarter of them had died—and even more of the natives: about one in three of them. One report said there was a death for every sleeper on the track. Most had died from the starvation diet, outbreaks of cholera, the injuries treatable but untreated, and the brutality of the guards—both Jap and Korean. Far worse than anything the Allies did.

And since then: What—it's years later and Japan has never admitted the atrocity. They've never apologised: not even to the poor 'comfort women' who were brought on barges to the camps for use by the Jap soldiers. Some girls wouldn't have been above twelve! He remembers the guards demonstrate with their fingers the 'jig a jig' they were about to enjoy. Probably they did it to make the prisoners jealous—but they were so underfed and ill they weren't interested in sex any more. That worried them— if they lived, would they be able to be proper men when they got back to their sweethearts and wives? Would they be able to father children?

Sam frowns. 'What if it was me who died, Ernie? Would you have been able to "move on" if you'd seen my brain fall in the mud? Would you?'

It's as if Ernie is with him, a steady hand on his shoulder, saying, 'Hey come on Sam! You know me—better than anyone does!' Sam nods. Yes, he does. Ernie, who died to save him, knew the world had to move on—just as it had. He was the sort who'd forgive and help make peace.

'I can't, Ernie,' he whispers. 'I can't forgive them. I admit you're right. It's the only hope in the long run. But forgiveness will have to be given by others. Peace can be too bloody dear.'

He looks around him: most of those who attend are young. A soaking wet boy smiles at him—he's blond like Ernie—and for once he smiles back. Good looking kid—confident too. Not cheeky like some. It's good the youngsters come—they're another generation to keep the memories of soldiers like Ernie alive.

It's nearly the end of the service now. Sam shivers, but the sun, just risen, breaks through the rain. A young soldier, head bared, is reading "For the Fallen" before the flag lowers and the few surviving diggers slope off to the pubs:

> '... They shall not grow old, as we
> that are left grow old:
> Age shall not weary them, nor the
> years condemn.
>
> At the going down of the sun and in
> the morning
> We will remember them.
>
> 'As the stars that shall be bright when
> we are dust,
> Moving in marches upon the heav-
> enly plain;
> As the stars that are starry in the time
> of our darkness,
> To the end, to the end, they remain.'

Futures Trader

I've arrived -- but I'm reluctant to leave the rental. The sound system's great and the car's warm—which in Mosgiel winters is as essential as breath. I look in the rear vision mirror to re-do my lipstick and straighten my hair. I'm shaking. Mum hasn't come to the front door yet but could be lurking behind those dingy net curtains in the lounge.

I hate these old brick houses. They're built to parallel the road and ignore the views, sun and wind. Mum's lounge is on the south side along with the master bedroom—the Master Bedroom. A mistress bedroom would sound much sexier but it's probably too cold in a south-facing bedroom to be sexy. "There'll be no hubba-hubba if you don't wear four jerseys and polyprop underwear" doesn't exactly entice. What would I know about that though?

The path to the door has aged since I saw it last; cracks and moss mosaic its surface. Shrubs have grown and unchecked hydrangeas narrow the path with their pale brown leaf litter.

Still, I haven't flown down here to look at the house.

I leave my suitcase in the car and move up the path onto the porch. The wind puts its hands up my skirt and tugs hard. It is Antarctic-cold and involuntarily I look at my fingers and remember the broken itchy chilblains I used to get when I lived here. My fingernails were bitten to the quick as a child so I look with satisfaction at their pink polished length now. I cup my face, struggling to warm it a degree above neutrality, then knock.

Nothing. My shoulders and neck stiffen. Has she forgotten? I slap the brass doorknocker hard onto its plate and hear slow footsteps make their way up the hall. Does she want to see me? When I phoned she sounded okay about it. The door opens widely.

'Hello dear,' she says. 'Do you want a cup of tea? I've got some ready.' Her face is pushed to within millimetres of mine so I dab a kiss on her cheek.

Tea! I look at Mum. She smiles warmly at me. Her hand flicks hair from her face. Her eyes are different somehow—and her mouth. The mouth that used to snarl and snap at me is soft and sort of loose. As I follow her into the narrow hallway I stare at her back; she's shrunk and she stoops. She wears an old grey cardigan, and her stockings or pantyhose, or whatever they are, sag around her calves and into her grubby slippers. She *shuffles*! I sit in the lounge and Mum goes to the kitchen.

Last time I was in this room sixteen years ago, Mum and I shouted abuse at one another. I shake my head.

Like many eruptions, this one started small.

'Your Auntie Rose is coming next week and the garden looks dreadful. Surely you could give up just one morning to tidy things up. Mow the lawns or weed the gardens by the front path... anything would help.'

'Mum, you don't understand. I've got my B. Com finals next week and need to do well! I can't take time off for anything else at all—it's not as if I flop about and watch TV or take off to a nightclub! I have to study.'

The argument escalated until Mum jabbed me in the chest, her normally quiet voice as loud as a jackhammer:

'I don't ask for much—just a little help now and then: Just your duty to your family. But you're so arrogant since you went to university. You don't care for any of us anymore!' Her lips almost disappeared and she strode onto the high ground of her religion. 'You are greedy! Yes you are!' as she saw me ready to protest. Her hand raised a stop sign. 'Greedy. Remember Matthew, Chapter 21 when Jesus overthrew the moneychangers and said, "Ye have made it a den of thieves!"'

Mum is like that—can quote slabs of the Bible at the drop of a moral standard. For a moment longer I kept quiet—I actually remembered this quotation because it always puzzled me why Jesus also overthrew the seats of those dove sellers. Doves, of all things! Symbols of peace and innocence!

'You treat us like dirt,' she wound down.

'My turn now Mum.' I was furious. 'If I seem greedy to you,' I yelled, 'it's because we've always been fucking poor!' I enjoyed seeing her face blanch at the expletive. 'When Dad died, did you ever get off your arse and earn money? No! We've lived like beggars. My childhood was totally stuffed up thanks to you!'

She was probably right about the garden—I could have had study breaks. But now I remember the thin frayed blankets I shivered underneath, the awful meals of mince served in a swamp of half-congealed fat. I wasn't allowed to learn the violin provided free from the school, because I would never continue with it. Ditto ballet. Ditto diving lessons… If I topped the class and came home with pride and a new book I was a show-off. If I failed a class it was because I wouldn't work hard and wouldn't stick to anything. I couldn't win.

I can't remember what it was like before Dad died—but afterwards we grimly fought our way through my childhood and adolescence… and shortly after that last battle I flew to Auckland and tried to forget home. The muscles in my neck are rigid as I think about it now. Why on earth have I come back?

The tea is tepid and tastes of dust. Mum sits as close to me as she can, leans forward from her chair and smiles her soft smile. She pats my hand. Has she missed me that much?

I tell her about my life. Cautiously I relate how successful my futures trading career is. I watch her to see if she stiffens up and her mouth makes the tight line but she nods—head on one side—interested. I tell her the fluctuating price of oil and gold has made the job harder but I'm still doing well. Very well. I tell her about the company I own and work for as a sole trader. No tirades from her about the Lord's vengeance or my personal sins yet.

Still carefully, I move further onto what was shaky ground for us years back. I tell her about the penthouse apartment I live in and others I've bought and rent out. North facing balconies, views, values that have doubled in a couple of years… I tell her how high rents are in Auckland and her face doesn't change. Has she used botox or something? Amazing!

'Have you a man in your life?' she asks. Is this criticism?

'No, I live alone.' No comment from her.

'Are you happy?' she asks, going to the centre of the problem. She looks worried about me.

This is like a dream: the dream of the mother I always wanted. Robbed of rationality, I sit on the carpeted floor at her feet.

'Happy?' I echo. 'Am I happy? Would you be if you looked like me? I'm an exact replica of the Venus of Willendorf: all tits and belly and thighs!' Not that Mum's likely to know about the Venus. Once though, such vulgarity would have brought a comment about my "foul mouth"—but nothing happens today. 'It'd be okay,' I continue, 'if I lived in Neanderthal times. Then, I would've been the most wanted woman in the cave—surrounded by babies.' Babies…

My breasts swell and ache each month just before menstruation. I imagine it's pretty much what they'd feel like if they were full of milk. What would it feel like to be suckled? I've sometimes squeezed my sore nipples hard and looked to see if by some miracle they contain milk. I can't help it. Each month I think: *"There goes another egg. How many have I got left? Are they any good?"* They damage with age—Downs Syndrome—other stuff.

Every time I go out to grab some McDonald's to eat, I see pregnant women everywhere. They all wear a Mona Lisa smile. If they wait in a queue they rub their bellies. If they walk down Queen Street they admire their swollen profiles in the window glass—while my fecund-looking body is an empty fat-filled fraud… What did someone say about menstruation? Yes—"the tears from a disappointed uterus." I want a baby, I want a baby, I want a baby, I WANT A BABY. My biological clock doesn't tick—it clangs like Big Ben. And I haven't even got a man—let alone a baby.

I can feel my face redden. Tears push out onto my cheeks and I shake with unexpected sobs. 'I want a baby, Mum, so badly, and a husband—I don't want to be a parent on my own. I'm thirty-eight now and time's running out and I'm fat and ugly and I sweat as I walk to the lift and I stink like rotting fish if I sit out in the sun…' I can speak no more for a time.

Her arms are around me; her tears mingle with mine as she pats my back and kisses my hair.

'You can't know what's around the corner my girl,' And she's right. She produces a box of tissues and I blow my nose loudly. I haven't cried for years but gradually the sobs slow and stop.

'I look like a great success up in Auckland. But I'm so miserable—I eat too much and drink too much and just look at me!' More tears. Mum doesn't try to tell me it's not true—she calls me her dear girl, and offers tissues and cuddles. Nothing in my life has changed but I feel a bit more optimistic.

Mum is tired—nods off. She looks frail. I go to the kitchen—it's the same as when I lived here: the china with the transfers worn off and the pots with lids missing the handles, tea towels you can see through. The paint on the walls hasn't changed either. Quietly, I go to the Mosgiel supermarket and bring supplies in for our dinner.

Later, in my narrow bed, warm thanks to the goose down duvet I brought with me, long forgotten memories of my childhood bubble through the barriers in my head. There was a trip to the beach with Mum and my brother Ken. We had a picnic there with a tartan blanket, a plastic beach ball thrown back and forth between us, sand crunched in my sandwich and sun bleached the sky. Mum tried to teach me to swim; one hand under my tummy she struggled to speak encouragement, while my frantic arm movements filled her mouth with salty water.

And there were kisses she scattered on my face each night—and the silly songs she made up about the day's events. I remember her laughing and laughing when we visited a farm and she got stuck in the mud. I was in her arms. She wore a striped blue jersey and I laughed with her. I must have only been about five then I guess. She was always there when I got home from school—made me do homework—bought books with her inadequate income. Why do I remember now?

For the next few days this peaceful life continues. Mum and I spend a lot of time together weeding to retrieve the garden spaces. The air, though cold, is clean air. Not like the overused Auckland air. My unexercised body protests—it is sore and stiff—but even in a few days it copes better with the walks, bends and tugs that gardening demands.

I notice Mum tires easily and often sits in a faded

deck chair as I work. When I have breath enough, we talk. Over and over again I talk about my life in Auckland and repeatedly she helps me. In return she tells me about her childhood. Stories I've never heard before. She lived on a dairy farm, helped with farm chores like looking after the hens, gardening and getting reluctant cows with waving, dung-spattered tails into equally dung-spattered bales for milking. Her Sundays were drab with a harsher religion than the one she used to try and tame my brother and me… I begin to see what shaped her—understand and like her more. She steadies me with gentleness, compassion and unconditional love.

About a week after my arrival Ken phones me from Christchurch. He's pleased I'm in his island. 'I'll come down next weekend,' he promises. 'I guess then we'll need to talk about what to do with Mum.'

'What do you mean? I mean, I know she's getting old—but other than that?'

'She won't be able to manage on her own much longer.'

'What's wrong with her? Is she ill?'

'Yes. Not bad physically but she's in the early stages of dementia.'

'I don't believe it! She's fine!'

'Del, listen. Has she called you by your name—even once?' She hasn't. As soon as I can I hang up. Dementia.

Mum dozes in the sunroom at the back of the house, an unread book on her lap. The room is chilly. Clouds have covered the sun and some large drops of rain dot the window.

'Mum,' I say quietly, 'Who am I?'

'You're my darling girl.' Her eyelids lower and she looks worried.

I walk away from her into the lounge. Self-pity swamps me: it's all a lie. Mum's only nice because she's going off her rocker. Smoke puffs out of the fireplace. Damp wood. It always happens. My eyes water. And now the rain pelts down—if it carries on for long the Taieri Plains will flood. I want to leave and not come back.

I feel so cheated and angry. It's as though the sixteen year gap has disappeared and the real Mum is the woman who disapproves of me. I curl into a corner of the old sofa—a spring pushes at my back. For ages—hours? I'm awash with disillusion. All the black thoughts about our relationship steal back into my brain. I chew my manicured nails. Mum doesn't come to find me.

I calm down only as a new thought comes to me. What if this week's mother is my real Mother? This, this caring woman who has supported me so well… What if this is the truth? Her failing brain is simply stripped down to the quintessential and loving woman she always was under the patina of poverty and religious bigotry… Of course. How silly of me not to see it! Of course that's it!

Energised, I plan our future. It'd be better for her to remain in her own house. Familiar surroundings. I could keep my apartment—or rent or sell it. Some of my money would make us comfortable. More sun and insulation in the house; light colours throughout; new clothes for Mum. I feel like Santa Claus.

It'd be as easy for me to work from Mosgiel as Auckland, given all my work is online. I'd ease off the hours—and still make enough to live well. It'd get hard, I guess, as she got worse. But I could afford help—a nurse when we needed one…

Then I hesitate. Is this what Mum would want? For once it is important.

Mum has appeared behind me—wandering—wanting a drink. I warm some milk in a pot, pour it into the only undamaged cup I can find in the cupboard, and sit beside her on the couch.

'Mum,' I say, 'would you like me to come home and live here with you?' Then I realise just how terribly, terribly much I need her to say yes.

Eagle Boy

Eagle Boy died yesterday. I saw the notices in the paper. I don't know whether to go to the funeral or not—but it stirs up memories. He was the sort of bloke you don't forget.

I knew him before he was an eagle: more an unfledged sparrow with arms and legs so thin his joints jolted the eye. We lived a couple of streets away from each other and went to the same school. Were we friends? More like mutual outcasts hiding from the herd. I wore glasses and, like Eagle Boy, was small and easily knocked about. We met in a patch of flax at the rear of the school playground hidden from the other kids—and hiding was about all we had in common then.

It was a basis though. We talked of revenge on the bullies—of how good it'd be to get them in a bear trap and leave them there to rot; or tie them up and pull out their eyelashes one by one; or push them off a cliff. We'd flex our arms and imagine the bulge of the muscles we'd have one day and we'd warmly wrap ourselves in the ideas. It made it all tolerable.

I was there when Eagle Boy saw his first eagle. We

were city kids and all went on a school camp near Mount Egmont—or Taranaki as it is now. Can't remember much but I do remember it was in the country—grass, bush, a river, clean cold air. And this eagle soared over the bush in the valley below our huts.

Eagle Boy asked the camp commander, or whatever he was, about the eagle. How did it fly like that? What was its proper name? What did it eat? Camp commander said it was an eagle doing a bit of gliding—it ate mice, rabbits, whatever. Nothing much. But it was the start of a passion for Eagle Boy.

Soon, he borrowed books about birds from the school library.

'It wasn't an eagle, Bob. It was a falcon—*Falco novae-seelandieae*. And listen to this: it's a hunter. It waits quietly then—Wham! Kills magpies and pigeons and everything.'

'It was beautiful,' I ventured.

Eagle Boy looked at me scornfully. 'Not *beautiful*—powerful and majestic.'

'Okay.'

I worried whether he was turning peculiar when I found him behind our flax flapping his arms like wings. Actually, I was scared the bullies would polish us both off if they saw him flapping away. I had to do something urgently.

'Do you think you're going to fly then,' I asked him.

'Don't be dopey, Bob. I just think it might strengthen my arms up. After all, eagles must be incredibly strong to be able to lift their body weight up. They're big birds.'

'Okay. But do you think you could do it at home? I think I see the bullies on the other side of the flax.'

He stayed skinny. But he got a more confident look in his eye. Some of the bullies stopped whacking him. I'd saunter along and copy the look as best I could. He didn't talk about eagles that much anymore.

Can't remember when I went to his place after school—high school by then—to do some homework. We went to his room. There, the eagle ruled. There, posters and paperweights and flags and coins and books and lamps and pictures of the moon landing craft jostled for space: all featured eagles. A Bible open at Jeremiah 49:22, vivid with red marker pen, was placed in a glass-fronted case like we all made at woodworking class. A virginal ashtray sat in the clutter with its American Eagle transfer glowing with unnatural colour… Even his bedcover was eagled.

Largest of all was a model of New Zealand's Haast Eagle—life sized. All three metres wingspan hung from his ceiling on wires. It was shaped in fibreglass I think. Painted up. He watched me looking.

'That was New Zealand's top predator. Sat in tall trees watching for prey then dropped on them at eighty k's an hour. Ate moa! Its beak was stronger than bone! Nothing could beat it.

'I made that model. It took months.'

'It would.' I felt uncomfortable. 'Why'd you collect all this stuff?'

His eyes slid about, hunting an escape. 'It'll get valuable,' he managed.

'Okay,' I said, and left it at that. But I knew he was lying. I wondered if he was ashamed of his obsession with birds, and whether he'd go on to uni and become an ornithologist, but that idea didn't seem to fit very well.

Once school ended, we didn't meet for years. I went on and did an engineering degree before doing the big OE. He did accounting I think. I was away from New Zealand more than ten years—Middle East, Europe, Asia—and came back to buy an engineering practice in Gisborne. I did all the usual things: loved, married, had two-and-a-half children.

During the slump of the late eighties, we were

hard-hit in Gisborne. Farmers had been struggling for a few years before the 1987 sharemarket crash: subsidies had been taken off in the Douglas budget of 1984—and that meant fewer dams, sheds and drainage schemes being built around our way. In 1987 too, the government formed the state corporations, and they promptly put off thousands of workers. A lot of the old forestry towns died right then and the foresters sought jobs in the cities. Of course the huge houses now dotting the Gisborne area weren't even a sparkle in a developer's eye, and public works like roads and bridges were delayed—along with my income. It was tough. I watched the papers to see how Eagle Boy was coping.

His life was played out in the news. He'd built up a huge business, by New Zealand standards anyway, and you knew it was a bad year for him if he didn't top the Rich List. He bought himself a villa in France, an apartment in New York and a high country farm near Queenstown. His cars and women, takeovers and boats were all grist to the gossip columnists' mill. How I envied him then. His life was full of glamour—even though most of the high flyers in New Zealand had well and truly had their wings clipped. I'd see pictures of him smiling at the races with his latest wife and the latest thoroughbred horse and the latest trotting Cup. I read the business pages and his businesses hardly faltered. I wished I could be that wealthy, that famous, and that free from worry.

But bankruptcy was as close to me as the scarf around my throat during the winter of 1989. It was a winter of landslides and rain and creditors pleading for their money. The bank manager would even invite me to breakfast at his expense and we'd go over the accounts and I'd grow ulcers.

I sat in my office day after day, rent unpaid, rolling a pen idly in my fingers. If only the phone would ring or some canny person who still had money would walk in and commission me to do something—anything.

Eventually I thought of approaching Eagle Boy for a loan on the basis of our long ago friendship. My debts would be nothing to him and getting them cleared would be everything to me.

I felt so bad, you see. It wasn't only our own lives—but lives of all the people I owed money to. Like many of the rural townswomen then, Mary had got herself a job—but working at the checkout of the local Four Square barely fed us and paid for child care. My landlord had only one office to let and when we couldn't pay the rent he couldn't pay his mortgage. I couldn't look him in the eye. And there was Tom. I kept him on for as long as I could, making tea instead of draughting, but when the work stopped altogether, he had to be put off. Although I gave him a great reference, he couldn't get another job anywhere.

So I wrote to Eagle Boy. I asked for a loan, and told him honestly about all my financial problems. I felt confident he'd give it to me—after all, he knew what it was like to feel fear and despair. We'd helped each other through the bullying and he'd remember that.

The reply I had from him was kind, in a way. "Bob," it began, "Nice to hear from you. It makes me think of the old days at school." So far so good, it seemed to me. "I have faith in you, Bob," it continued. "So much so that I will lend you the money you want. I know you well enough to know you can pull through this difficulty and repay me." I was elated. A loan document accompanied the letter. It offered me all I needed—but at 32.5% interest per annum: Penalty interest even in those times. He wrote more, but at that point, I admit it now, I cried.

He was right though, to have faith in me. And in a weird kind of way his letter spurred me to action. Somehow the bank manager continued to help me, and I carried on. Since there was no ordinary engineering work, I started working on inventions designed to help disabled children learn to walk. Our eldest son, Billy, had been born with a shrivelled stump of a leg and his discomfort and disability made me develop callipers for him. This started me off in a new direction; a business in medical engineering. It became successful—the callipers I made look primitive now, but gradually I made better ones and branched out into lasers and robotics and so on. I paid all my debts, times got better, and now I have a business I love working in, selling my products all around the world. It pays me very well.

After declining Eagle Boy's offer, our lives were so separate it was a real surprise when he turned up in my office on his own. His brand-new 2006 Maserati was parked outside. That would've set him back a bit. Clothes as you'd expect too: Rodd and Gunn casuals. The body inside the clothes was still a weed though. Thin, tense. A bony face made his hooked nose seem too big.

We talked uneasily—catch up stuff. He'd just bought a big vineyard near Gisborne. Had three wives over the time… Cursed them all. Had two kids, living with their mothers. I felt as though he'd come for a reason but he couldn't say what it was, and I couldn't guess it.

We walked through my factory. I had ten design engineers working with me and showed Eagle Boy the dreams on paper and the prototypes and the final products. A robotics engineer showed off a new machine he hoped would help those with spinal injuries to move.

'But this is what I'm most proud of,' I enthused as we walked into another section. It looked a mess. It always did. 'This is where we adapt the expensive developed products to send to third-world countries. See? The callipers I made for Billy all those years ago have been stripped down to the basics. They work and they're comfortable and we have a Trust now that sends them in thousands to countries plagued with land mines. This is the part of the factory I work in whenever I can get away from the administration stuff. All the normal sales of product to hospitals subsidises this. It's the best, most exciting work! When I retire, I'll still work here.'

Eagle Boy forced a smile, but I could see he wasn't listening. 'You remember school—the flax?' he managed as we walked back to my office.

'Yep. Who said childhood is the best time of our lives. Wasn't my best time. The years since the '89 crash have been my best years.'

'Yeah?' he said.

'Yeah. What could be better than now?' I replied. 'I love what I do. Got a great wife and kids. You can catch fish around here and the local wine is bloody marvellous. I'm sure as hell not a big shot like you though—oh boy, have you done well! 'Business Man of the Year' isn't in it?'

He nodded. His eyes roved my small office—tucked into a corner of the factory—his hands flapped then gradually subsided and his shoulders slumped. Then he straightened up.

'Yes I have. Bloody well.' His face looked hard. 'Earned every bloody cent of it.' He left soon after.

And now he's dead and I wonder what he came for and it's too late to find out. I will go to his funeral though.

It's a large funeral with a big and glossy coffin for an important man. Too big a coffin for the boy I remember. The service is long and impersonal: a lot of religion and a lot about his businesses. Don't find out anything much about Eagle Boy there.

After the service I stand outside the funeral place and talk to as many people as I can. One of his kids and two of his wives are here. The wives keep away from one another. The kid stands beside his mother shuffling his feet. He looks a bit like Eagle Boy. When I try to find out what Eagle Boy was like, the wives smile twin thin smiles and tell me nothing.

Men in suits tell me he was a great business man; nothing particular about how he got there, but he got there. A hard man who knew what he wanted.

He made a fortune with a private equity company he owned. A red-faced man says: 'He wouldn't have been able to go back to that ex-communist country near Russia though—can't remember its name. Once he'd bought the railroad there, he sold off all the maintenance stock—all the rails and so on—then on-sold the Rail for about $120 million profit. Caused a huge political stink. People don't forget that do they. I heard there were even death threats…'

Another man rubs his hands together as he praises Eagle Boy: he'd come to a charity auction raising money for a sanctuary for endangered native species in Wellington, and had given hundreds of thousands of dollars for its erection. They'd named it after him. 'Marvellous,' he raved, 'a busy man like that to take time to come to our auction! And, do you know, he bid on items, won, paid for them, gave them back for re-sale to the second bidder. The only thing he kept was a Don Binney painting of the Haast Eagle.'

A rough looking man standing on the edge of the crowd smells of booze. He says the Eagle Boy ruined him by underselling heavy machinery in New Zealand until his business failed. He isn't sorry Eagle Boy has died. He couldn't quite say why he'd turned up at the funeral. Curiosity, probably.

One woman, smoking urgently, lips and nails blazing red, has eyes untouched but mouth sad for the occasion. She says he was a lovely man. Just lovely. Very rich. Very, very rich—as though the loveliness and the wealth were somehow related.

'Sad isn't it,' she carries on, then her voice drops, 'to think of such a nice man killing himself.'

A man taps me on the arm and asks if I am Bob Martin. I nod.

'I'm one of the area managers in the company. He said something about you a couple of weeks ago. Asked me to ask, if I ever met you, whether you still remembered the eagle. What did he mean?'

I shake my head. That was probably what he wanted to talk about. I smell the damp bush, hear the river running over stones, and see the 'eagle' circling on the currents of air above us all. What would his life have been like if he had never seen it fly? That one wasn't even a bloody eagle at all... to think I envied him — wanted his life. Now I can't believe how sorry for him I am... and yet... his values...

I walk away from the crowd and phone Margaret and the kids to tell them I'll be on the five o'clock flight. I tell them how much I love them. I can't wait to get home.

A Perfect Day

My kayak slides effortlessly across the worn carpet in my lounge, but as soon as I lift it past the bi-fold doors and over the deck to the lawn, I inch my pace so I don't stumble, and then hoist the kayak high: It is more valuable than me.

Have I got all I need? I have my fishing lines, my two silver and paua earrings, a landing net, life jacket, paddle and attachment: Must not lose paddle. And the old life-jacket is the only one I have—hope it works. I put it on then stow all the other gear into the waterproof hatches fore and aft and screw the lids tight.

Downhill now, the kayak slips lightly over the grass—so no risk of scratches. Kayak on kikuyu. Sounds like a meal—or the name of a café. I smile as I walk and the cushion of kikuyu nests my bare feet. The sky lightens and a slim sliver of cream slides under the cloud on the horizon in the east. Lovely—but I must hurry now. Funny to be in a hurry when I can only guess the time!

The steep bank makes it easy to float the kayak and paddle off, and because I'm not an expert paddler I'm glad it's a light sit-on-top kayak. It's a stable platform, not a trap like the pro ones with the skirt you wear and the hull shaped to capsize with the whim of a paddle. I head north. Although I can see the tops of many of the old canopy trees—totara, rimu, kohekohe, taraire, kauri—they are all dead. I paddle well away from them. The tall dead trees don't worry me—there are lots of live ones higher up, but shorter ones might tip me out or damage my boat. When I am well clear, I head east. The Poor Knights float enticingly on the horizon—but I won't go that far. The weather there is dodgy. The sea right now though, is satin, and the smoothest patches of water gleam like pale blue ribbons paralleling the line of cliffs and hills. There's no wind. No immediate storm. No rain. It is hot already. The ripples from the paddle ruffle the satin and the kayak makes a 'v' in the water which stretches to reach the shore behind me.

I'm over the place where the shoreline used to be, and when I throw out the anchor it flies from me to slide into the sea without a splash. I tie an earring to the slippery nylon line, throw it over the side, and jiggle it so the paua flashes and fires enticingly in the clear water. Nothing comes to the lure. It still flashes ages later: An underwater lighthouse. Perhaps it is warning the fish...

My kayak seat is comfortable and I lean back. Now, I decide. Now is the time. I reach behind me and retrieve a velvet-wrapped antique crystal glass and a well-aged bottle of Te Mata Coleraine from the hatch at the rear of the kayak, ease the cork out effortlessly, and pour. The sun turns the wine into a radiant red beacon. I sip until it is gone. The tastes fill my mouth. My tongue luxuriates. My mind is still.

It is so beautiful here, even if I haven't caught anything yet. My hand trails in the water. It is warm. I am content. 'Just a perfect day, the animals in the zoo...' I sing... If I peer over the side of the kayak I can see Goldminer's Beach through the water. Although it is now drowned, the white sand is there—still rippled by the sea. How long will it take new beaches to form on the hillside? A few years? A thousand?

Still no fish. I decide to give up for a while and swim instead. With my clothes off I dive deep and the cool water rushes over my skin. I fly. I weigh nothing at all. My visibility is excellent as I near the bottom.

When my hand touches the sand and searches for shellfish I can't feel any. Ahead I see just one—a huge conical gastropod. When I pick it up with both hands its shell dissolves into the sea in a whitish-brown puff and its naked grey body writhes and collapses. I wipe the slimy remains off my hand once I get to the surface, then climb awkwardly into the kayak. I'm not surprised about the shellfish. The ocean pH has changed. I remember my chemistry lessons from high school—chalk and acid...

Unexpectedly, I feel like the naked gastropod: vulnerable, soft-skinned and an easy target. Quickly and clumsily I pull on my knickers, shorts, T-shirt and life jacket. The sea warns: "WAIS, WAIS," it sings. I stare about me. It is still. No wind. No change since I came out here this morning—but the sea is more strident. "The WAIS," it moans in a low voice. "The WAIS is coming."

What the hell does it mean? I shiver as I look at the sky. Black-backed gulls whirl over my head in a great flock. They dim the sun and remind me of vultures.

It's hard to get the anchor up. I tug at it—pull urgently at the warp. Is it wrapped around something? Has the anchor wedged between rocks? I cannot free it. But I must not lose it. As I prepare to take my clothes off for another dive, I pull hard once more and this time the anchor comes up so suddenly I almost fall into the sea. Like a freed prisoner, the kayak rushes me away from the land. I paddle as fast and deep as I can toward home. But it is futile. What is moving the kayak?

I look back toward our place. Whole skeletons of

dead trees are uncovered. Dead paddocks are covered in mud and rock. Our house looks so small… The land shrinks as I tear away from it.

Out past the Poor Knights: Out into the blue depths of a truly Pacific Ocean. The sea sucks me southwards. There are no ripples caused by the kayak despite the speed at which we travel. I cling to its sides. What will happen to me? Soon there is nothing to be seen but sea. The WAIS it roars. The WAIS is nearly here. My heart thumps wildly. What the fuck is the WAIS?

It is freezing and I am cold to my marrow. I hug myself, and brace my legs along the sides of the kayak. A fall into these icy seas…

In the distance now I see a bluish white line. My eyeballs freeze in the southern wind and I don't think I can close the lids. 'WAIS, WAIS, WAIS,' drums my head — adding to the chaos. As we rush on, I see the line is a wall of ice thousands of metres high, kilometres long.

The kayak hits a submerged iceberg. I fly high into the air. Surely this is death. But over the ice shelf I fly. My arms, feathered with thousands of icicles, are outspread and keep me aloft.

Oh! This is the most precious place I've ever seen. Blue and white ice glows with the sun behind. Rare rocks are patterned with ancient lichens. At the edge of the ice sheet Adelie, Chinstrap, Gentoo and Emperor penguins stand in military lines. They stare at the sea.

The sun blazes an arc welder's flame onto the ice. Vast chasms with waterfalls of melt water appear. The ice shelf shears from its rock base. It falls into the sea with a roar of protest. The penguins can't escape.

My wings melt too: Icarus. I plummet from the sky and a tsunami, packed with a tumble of ice, snatches me; pounds me. I gulp water, then air. 'The WAIS,' I scream. The WAIS!' My heart erupts from my chest…

'Wake up!' John tugs on my arm.

'The WAIS!' I start. His arms try to cuddle me. I kiss him hard then push him away and run into the children's room. They're both there, safe. I want to rip them from their beds and hug them. Hungrily, I adjust their blankets. Their eyelashes are long and their skin smooth: their faces are relaxed—pink and trustful in the early morning light. Logan has a Harry Potter book under his hand. Emma, only twenty months old, cuddles a large toy dog.

I go to the windows in our lounge. The trees are still alive. The huge epiphytes in their branches are lush and green. The wetlands have not drowned. The sea, blue and beribboned, is as harmless as a pond. The shed at the bottom of the hill where we keep the kayaks has not flooded. And the white beaches are still beaches with shellfish still protected by their shells. Tears come. Weak with relief I sit down on the couch. We're safe—aren't we?

Beside me, where I left it last night, is a crumpled copy of one of my New Scientist magazines open at yet another article about climate change: "The IPCC team also sidelined findings from the British Antarctic Survey. BAS researchers say that the Antarctic Peninsula is warming faster than almost anywhere on the planet. They have documented a sharp decline in sea ice around the peninsula, and warn that the giant West Antarctic ice sheet (WAIS) is "unstable and contributing significantly to sea level rise." Elsewhere, predictions said it would raise the sea level by five or six metres if it collapsed… Five or six metres! Just that part of Antarctica—not all the ice on the planet! If it all melts, sea levels will rise seventy or more metres. We aren't safe. I get up and stride around the lounge.

How can I protect my children? Always as I grew up, amongst all the uncertainties the Earth was sure. I would die, but my children and their children would live on… "As it was in the beginning, is now and ever shall be, World without end". No childhood vespers can comfort me now.

I see the ice sheet crash, and see the water speed to

the shore. Great waves smash the puny low-lying ports, topple the vain sky scrapers and fling locomotives as easily as a juggler tosses balls. I see bodies tumbling over and over… my heart races again.

And I cannot stop: I see the land shrivel and die. There are no birds or cows or sheep. No grass or crops. Only a brazen sun cracking the Earth apart. Worst: An aged and desiccated couple with eyes the colour of Logan's are holding dry earth in their hands instead of food. They ask why we let it happen.

I know as each day passes and each study is published, the probability of climate change strengthens: The predictions of the time it will take to become fatal have shrunk from centuries to decades. Where only a few years ago an increase in temperature of just 0.8 degrees Celsius was predicted, it's touching one degree already. I've read some of the studies on atmosphere, species extinctions, ocean change—and dozens of other aspects—for years. Climate change has begun and we have caused it. Only we can stop it.

Who wants to think about that? It's overwhelming—frightening. I feel helpless. It's so huge. And the earth looks just as healthy as it always did—sure its temperature is up a bit and it's more restless—but it would be hard for someone who doesn't know to recognise how serious its illness is. The planet's always been pretty erratic.

I've been comfortable concealing the threat in the daily clutter and rush of work and family. I heard the other day New Zealanders now work hours second only to Japan. How can I get time to think about anything when I work far more than forty hours a week as a radiologist and strive to be a good parent and lover as well? How can anyone?

I stop at the windows again and look at the unutterably beautiful Earth. From here I can see a tiny portion of its great arc. I breathe deeply: In—two, three, four. Out—two, three, four. As my anguish eases, my resolve grows.

It is not too late yet. With paper and pen from my office I sit back on the couch. I will write a list of things our family can do...'Now,' I say out loud. 'Now we must change.' There are no excuses. I start writing—but Emma is at my side—warm and cuddly. She needs breakfast. Logan's soccer will start soon and then there is shopping and the house to clean. This afternoon my parents are arriving—must buy wine. Somehow I've got to write a report before Monday and get online to pay another instalment on the car; due yesterday. Is that a nit on Logan's head? Surely not—but Emma's just had them. I stand up to go and get the magnifying glass from my office drawer.

The list will be safe on the rack under the coffee table. I'll look at it later; as soon as I can. But this time—this time it's for sure.

Sole Mate

I love Michael more than any woman has loved any man. How do you describe that? I can say we've been married for a year but that could mean anything. I can try to tell you how attractive he is to me: every hair in the cowlick he tries to dampen down every morning, every smile-wrinkle, each finger and toe, his skin smell—and the laugh that ends in a snort. It's all true but trite. My love is grander than that. Like any druggie, I get a rush in his arms—the arms I will live for and die in—but that doesn't say anywhere near enough. I would... I would kill for him. That's nearer but still not there.

'What are you thinking about, Michael?'

'Nothing. Nothing much at all.'

He is though. The pupils of his eyes change. A second ago they were huge, but with my question they shrink to shut me out.

'Ours is the most perfect marriage in the world, isn't it.'

'Mmm.' He pads off to the kitchen to get a drink of water. I watch. I always watch. I know how his long fingers grasp the glass, and how his Adam's apple will move, and how his eyes will close as he gulps the drink.

I know, too, we must share everything to make a perfect marriage—every thought and every memory. There'll be no misunderstandings then. Not like my Mum and Dad, who put on masks then skated blind over the thin ice of their relationship. It's more difficult than you'd think though. Michael's not easy to understand.

It's not that he's secretive. It's more that he's so intelligent; far more intelligent than me, or should that be 'I'? I'm not a complete idiot. I got my librarian's degree okay. (Well, marginally, if I'm honest.)

Everyone reminds me how lucky I am now—even my own mother. And his head of department raves on: "Michael? Top man in his line. Shouldn't be surprised if one day he got the Nobel Prize for Mathematics—his topological studies are far ahead of anybody else's." I hardly know what topology is but try to keep up. Studying maths is hard for me, and the topological formulae on distorted surfaces just send me to sleep. Also, my job at the library doesn't leave me a lot of time to study.

Michael's back from the kitchen.

'What are you thinking about now Michael?'

'Nothing Aurelia.' He sighs.

'Really?'

'Brain's on screen-save.'

Skull to skull: two layers of hair, two layers of skin, two layers of bone, and two brains less than a centimetre apart right now. We are sunbathing head-to-head at the edge of our very own pool in the back yard of our very own new and heavily mortgaged home. Michael's brain is a PET scanned image: sparking and glowing rainbow colours as it roams its own universe. My brain is dull and neuron-grey—intense colours fire only when I think of him. Two brains—not one; encased in impenetrable shells. Not really married. I want more than this.

'What are you thinking about, Michael?'

'Why do you always ask?'

'I'm scared of space between us. I want to feel at one with you.'

'Okay. I'm afraid I'll only bore you but here goes… I was wondering about the chlorine in the pool and what that other cleaning system was. It might be better.'

He could be thinking that. How would I know? I wriggle around next to him and lean up on one elbow. He's relaxed and hot—his nipples dissolving into the thick layer of sunscreen lotion I've smoothed all over his body. But he's frowning slightly. His brain is working on something and I have no idea what it might be. I kiss the frown and try to smooth it off with my fingers.

He rolls onto his side and kisses me.

'What's it like surviving marriage for one whole year?' Emily and I are sorting books for shelving.

'It's wonderful. Michael and I are so close.' I feel uneasy as I lie; yet by ordinary standards our marriage is wonderful. Our sex life is great; we share hobbies and values and a crooked-tailed tabby cat we found cowering in our vegetable garden one day… Michael is generous and loving—modest and calm. But more and more I need to know him as no other woman has known a man. He's becoming uncommunicative when I query his thoughts. Is it because he thinks I won't understand? Is he changing his mind about me?

I cuddle a book to my chest and picture him curled up in the bay window seat with Rhubarb purring loudly in his lap. He often strokes the cat absentmindedly and stares out of the window into the park next door. Sometimes he smiles; sometimes he scowls; sometimes he even flicks his hand impatiently and starts to talk to himself. How hard I listen then, to sieve the half-articulated syllables for sense. It's no good though. I cannot know all he is thinking about.

Emily is speaking—holding a book for me to see.

'New Age spiritual stuff. Weirdly popular isn't it?'

'Mmm.'

'Look at this one on out of the body journeys. Mr Warwick borrows every book like that. He must be crazy. I've just had to tell him he can't borrow it again for a while. Let someone else have a turn. Not as if it's a new book either. It was published back in 1971!'

'What's out of the body travel supposed to be?'

'Oh, you know—where people say they have an astral body they can use while they're asleep and they travel through space and look at stuff... Mr Warwick swears he's done it.'

I take the book. It falls open at page ninety-six. I read: *"The only explanation I can think of is that I, fully conscious of living and being 'here,' was attracted to and began momentarily to inhabit the body of a person."*

It is a sign. Surreptitiously, I borrow the book.

Three months of hard practice and I think I've got the basics learned. When I do the relaxation exercises I get vibrations, just as Monroe's book said I would. Sometimes I see a perfect ring of blue flames travel up and down around my body. They start like a damp fire—but soon settle into a rapid rhythm and spark. It amazes me they don't hurt. I haven't escaped from my body yet but it's very exciting. I haven't told Michael either. I'm going to surprise him when I get it right—probably tonight.

Last night it almost happened. I started to leave my body but became so exhilarated and aware that I sort of fell back in. Tonight I'll do better. Once I enter Michael's head, there'll be no more need for words. Everything in his mind will become part of me—even the topology. Once he knows what I can do, I'll teach him how to enter my mind, and our union will be complete.

I can't control my astral body! A week ago I used the countdown technique and before I reached thirty-one, the vibrations started up. I floated easily out of my body and could look down and see it, curled around Michael's back. But instead of being able to enter his mind, I shot through the roof of the house and out into complete blackness. Something like rough hands grabbed at me. I screamed, silently—like Munch's painting—and somehow that sent me back into my body—back into bed with Michael. I haven't dared try again until now.

Relax. Breathe slowly in and slowly out. One… two…

'Michael,' I think as I leave my body. 'Michael Robert Johnson!'

As easily as slipping on a glove, I slide into Michael's mind. I wait for revelation. For a long time there is nothing other than a slight electrical hum like that of well-balanced turbines spinning. My astral body is quiet and alert. My physical body lays still, a flaccid doll that waits to be inflated by my returning mind.

Thoughts come like bubbles released from a newly opened bottle of champagne. Michael groans and his eyeballs begin to move rapidly. He's dreaming.

I am in his dream, in the centre of a long red satin gown with a skirt that is the universe. There is no sky, no land, no sea—no other living things. Michael appears. Now there is just Michael and the dream 'I'. His face is close to mine, his eyes dark, and he proffers a single red rose. This is wonderful! How he must love me. We stare into each other's faces, breathing deeply. Our skin glows in the reflected light of the satin. It is so beautiful. I didn't realise… He stands on the dress as I accept the rose and reach for Michael with my arms. He is enfolded. When I move, I pull the dress from under his feet, so we fall together into the billowing layers of cloth. Michael's face is soft and sensuous and he strokes the satin and smiles. I stand up and watch, never taking my eyes off him as the red material moves like the tide onto the beach. It piles up in shimmering heaps onto Michael, whose smile dissolves into a grimace and then a cry.

'No more!' he screams to me. 'It's getting too heavy!' The red tide moves over his head and he is gone.

I cannot find him. My tears spill. I return to my body to find my pillow is wet. I cannot understand the dream. What happened? What can it mean? I do not sleep for the rest of the night.

There's no way I can ask Michael about it. He probably won't remember anyway. I'm not sure what to do next. Wonder whether I should tell him about my astral travels. But he'll laugh at me and demand proof. He's scientific, not intuitive. He won't understand.

'It was a dream,' I say to myself, 'just his crazy dream.' But now I'm scared to trespass on his deranged sleeping mind.

For a full two weeks I've considered what to do next. It seems that for now I can only bathe in Michael's stream of consciousness rather than access his stored memories. Still, that will be enough to go on with. I have made a decision: I'll enter his logical daytime mind. It's the only hope I have for fully understanding him.

Today Emily keeps asking me what's wrong. My mind isn't on my job, that's for sure. The sooner I do this, the better. Get back to normal. Why am I so reluctant? It will be wonderful—historic too: the first true marriage of minds and the first pair to overcome existential loneliness.

I tell Emily I'm not feeling well and go home at morning teatime. Michael is at work. The house is quiet. I grab his dressing gown from the floor in the bedroom and lie down with it cuddled to my face. I feel his smell will help me re-enter his brain.

It takes a long time to relax. Sunshine pokes around the dark curtains. Rhubarb jumps on me until I have to put her outside and ignore her mewing to be let back in. Breathe in, I say to myself… and out…

I use the lift-out method to leave my body. I mentally shout Michael's name, and once more am inside his body and brain. There is no quiet hum of turbines today.

Michael thinks: '…then I'll hand the paper to Anderton. I'll say it quietly: "I believe I'm able to determine in all situations whether two given geometric figures or point sets are homeomorphic." Nothing else. Blow him away!' Visions of money and kudos flutter and fly. His feet do a brief arrhythmic dance around his desk and his brain is ecstatic. Then x's and y's and a's and b's and numbers occupy his head. I can now understand them, but find it boring. I wonder if I can yawn in my astral body? And would my physical body yawn too? Hold on, he's thinking about something else…

'Twenty minutes to the meeting with Anderton… nearly ready… must phone Aurelia so's we can invite the Andertons over next Saturday…' I'm only a tiny asteroid in his universe. In a moment he's back to tapping paper into a neat stack on the desk and stapling it ready for the meeting. His mind whirrs with departmental politics.

I listen for as long as I can bear: for hours. I learn about an itch in his ear, an itch in his genitals for the departmental secretary, Michelle, and a worldly itch for fame through mathematics.

I find too, that this time I am surrounded by his fears and memories. They crowd me. He fears Isaac might beat him up the scientific ladder but thinks this scientific paper will crush him. The cowlick I love might turn into a whirlwind bald spot. I find he's scared of spiders! He's always teasing me because I'm terrified of them. Concerns about his flatulence and indigestion compete with worries about a flea he discovered on Rhubarb… His mind is full of monsters of all sizes.

I am relieved to return to my own body. Slowly I get up, let Rhubarb back in and settle down in the window seat with a mug of coffee to help me think. Michael's work — had he solved something that mattered? Probably.

I certainly didn't realise he feared Isaac. I thought they got on well. And Michelle—I've met a Michelle in the department working as a secretary. But does Michael want to make love to her? Would he? And all that plotting and pettiness! This is not my Michael.

I can't bear it. Maybe the astral travel was simply a dream. False. But my head hurts… I sigh. Was the dream my passion for Michael? All untrue? A tear slips onto my cheek and I brush it away impatiently. Michael will be home soon.

I look into my yellow mug—nearly empty now. It's not the only yellow mug I've owned. Dad dropped and broke the first one, patterned with blue forget-me-nots, when I was about six I guess. We were all in the kitchen after dinner and mum was drying the dishes using a faded tea towel with an upside down map of the world where New Zealand dominated. My job was to take the dried dishes from her and put them away on wooden shelves. The only sound for a time was water splashing in the sink.

Dad stopped washing to look at Mum and say, 'Think I'll pop out tonight. Dave's in town and I said I'd meet him later.'

'Pub. Again. That's where you're going isn't it?'

'Yes.' Dad scowled.

Mum's lips thinned to colourlessness. But she didn't say a thing more. She turned away from him, dropped the tea towel onto the varnished bench and left the kitchen. Dad washed the remaining dishes and slapped them into the drainer. My mug missed, and shattered on the tile floor.

Dad followed mum into the lounge, where she had put the TV on and then slumped into the old armchair. She knitted viciously with large grey needles.

'I'll be off then.' Mum ignored him.

'Bitch,' he muttered as he left…

Not unusual for mum and dad. I think I only remember it because of the mug.

So is this the future for Michael and me? Or will I be able to look honestly at him and love him anyway. Perhaps I was wrong to want to know everything about him. After all, there are things about me that I try to hide as well. My ignorance for one…

Maybe it will be okay. If he's just a flawed human—well so am I. The knots in my stomach loosen a little. Perhaps we are pretty much equal. (Me– equal with Michael! There's a thought.) I don't know though…

Michael walks in the door, and stops to pat the cat on the head. He smiles and kisses me and I hardly notice. When he gets himself coffee and joins me in the window seat I am silent. I try to understand what it all means. Michael stares at me. I wonder what's going on in his brain—then stop. I block out today's memories. I'm not ready to talk about them yet.

'What are you thinking about, Aurelia?'

I force a smile and stretch my arms above my head. 'Nothing much,' I reply. 'Brain's on screen-save.'

Through a Lens

Her hair attracts me: it's black and wavy and I'd like to photograph it. She's in a corner of the hide at Taiharuru Estuary and I'm here, like the others, to photograph bird life.

I plant my camera ready to gather godwits. The telephoto lens is an extravagance but at least I know, despite the drizzle, I'll get first-rate pictures.

An hour passes: The rain increases. No godwits—and no-one left in the damp hide other than the woman and me. She's angled unsociably—shoulders a barricade as she stares at the rocky junction of ocean and estuary. Her full lips droop; her black-lashed eyes are intent and almost unblinking; her slender hand holds crumpled tissues. She is a beautiful romantic figure.

A godwit lands and promptly plunges its long up-turned bill into the mud. 'There's one!' I blurt out, and photograph it feeding.

She doesn't answer—just gazes at the still estuary. Why's she here? She's Māori. Perhaps one of her tupuna died near here. I see Goldie's waka splinter on rocks. The arm of a young toa rises, falls, and disappears—Aue, aue!

But maybe she grieves for land lost—or perhaps this is a sacred place... Her head turns. Will she look at me? My eyes drop to the belly surfing my trousers. No, not me. I hear squelching footsteps.

The toa of my imagination strides from nowhere to the woman, whose eyes flash warning.

'All right. I'm sorry. Satisfied?' His voice is jagged and defiant.

'Whatever,' she says. I wish she'd smile.

He glares at me as though I have no right to be there; no right to overhear.

'My wife,' I stammer. 'We had a fight about this lens... Um... Whatever... Nothing's that...'

They stare at each other and his eyebrow raises.

I shrug, grab my camera quickly, and leave the hide, then smile: They're laughing and apologising.

Together.

Summer Roses

It is 3am. I cannot sleep. I must write.

Gloria sleeps just fine—normally she's still asleep when I leave for work. From the small light I've put on in the hall I can see her clearly. She sprawls on her back with her breath expelling in barely audible puffs and, surprisingly, in middle age, she's still a good-looking woman. It's futile, but I do wish we'd...

Never mind. I'll make myself a good strong cup of coffee and then I'll start writing. Now, if Gloria was like Susan... though Gloria was once perfect. I was so much in love. Wouldn't even let me touch her breasts until we married. And only for a short time afterwards, come to that. I mean, I understood her tiredness when Richard was little, but it's got worse over the years.

Where're the coffee beans? I hate instant coffee. The smell alone is enough to put you off. Trouble is, Gloria leaves the kitchen in a mess and moves stuff around so I can't find things. I even labelled the shelves in the pantry for her. Didn't work. Here's the coffee—right behind a label stating "Breakfast Cereals".

Susan keeps things in the office immaculate.

Immaculate. She came into my office three times today, wearing that white blouse and navy skirt. Lovely ankles.

It is 3am again. I can't sleep. I must write.

It's not as though not sleeping the whole night through is abnormal. I used to worry about it of course. Everyone expects to have eight hours sleep a night.

But I started reading about it. Astronauts before a flight—a time when they'd need their wits about them for sure—have only five hours. I'm no genius, but most intelligent men don't sleep much—a couple of naps, then on to fight the next battle or invent the next machine. Was it Napoleon Bonaparte who said "six hours sleep for a man, seven for a woman and eight for a fool"? Gloria must be getting well over ten hours. The number of times I've suggested she see a doctor about it—but she says that's just the way she is.

She's changed so much. She used to iron my shirts, see my dinner was cooked and cope with the tradesmen, but now she gets me to do the shopping on the way home from work—and the house and garden are a mess. She's become so static, and seems to spend all the time she's not sleeping watching soaps on TV.

I just wish she'd go out and get a job now Richard's left home. It'd broaden her out mentally, and we could do with the extra money. It's my fault in a way. I said I wanted her to stay home with Richard to give him a good start and she did: She made healthy lunches, saw his clothes were smart and picked him up to take him wherever he wanted to go. But he's got his own car now and his own life studying archaeology at uni.

Lately, when I arrive home, I find myself tugging at my shirt collar as though it's too tight: Saturday mow the lawn and visit Gloria's mother, Sunday is roast dinner, Thursday's pay day—you know. Last night I tried putting my hand up Gloria's skirt. But all she said was, 'For God's sake Robert, stop that. Can't you see I'm straining the vegetables?' I've often daydreamed about leaving her, but I'm scared to be alone. So is this what the rest of my life is going to be like?

Compensation: right now my job seems more attractive. I'm beginning to wonder about Susan. I noticed when she came into my office today that she smiled and looked into my eyes nearly all the time. Surely... I mean, I'm fifty-four years old and she's about Richard's age. Mind you, I keep in good shape: work in the garden regularly and sometimes go for a bit of a jog or mow the lawns.

It's always exactly 3 o'clock. I creep from the bedroom into the bathroom for a pee before going downstairs where I must write. I look in the mirror: my unshaven face looks pale and the dark bags under my eyes give me the sad look of a bloodhound. What can Susan see in me? For I am beginning to think she — how can I put this — wants me? I turn my head slightly. Yes, there's a bit of grey hair. Distinguished?

'Extinguished,' Gloria said when I showed her. But perhaps Susan likes older men. More experienced, more to offer. I mean, today she stopped and chatted when she brought some files that needed my attention. And she played with a curly bit of the blonde hair that fell across her face. Now that's significant: she curled it around her index finger quite deliberately while looking at me and chatting on about her parent's bach at Whitianga. Then she smoothed her skirt. Courtship gestures. Naturally, I responded with a bit of preening myself.

But what if I'm wrong? And what if I'm not? What'd it be like to kiss her over and over again? To press my lips hard onto hers and undo the blouse... What would her skin feel like? Cool? Warm and moist? It'd be smooth: Susan has no skin defects that I can see. What would she enjoy? I could read up on it: Somewhere we've got a book. Then again, what if I couldn't get an... It could happen. I'd die if it did. Hell! But in the anxiety of the situation...

Oh damn! Then there's Gloria. What if she found out. She's already as jealous as I don't know what. I believe she checks up on me; makes sure I stay alone at motels on business trips. Up 'til now she's had no cause to worry.

It'd be the end of the marriage. I'm sure of that. She'd never give me another chance. How often she's said there's more to marriage than sex: loyalty, steadiness, parental responsibility. How often she's called wives 'stupid' if they forgave a husband who strayed. Strayed. What a stupid word for what I'm feeling: compelled more like. My whole body is awake and sensitised.

I bought new underwear yesterday. It took Gloria no time at all to notice.

'What are these ridiculous undies? You're no Superman.' she scowled and held them up as though I needed to explain.

'You know I get a rash in summer,' I scowled back.

She walked near to me and sniffed derisively.

'You got a cold or something?' I asked. She raised one eyebrow but didn't say anything else thank goodness.

I take off the grey striped pyjamas that make me feel like a prisoner and pull on the underpants: they feel wonderful and sensuous—designed to emphasise my masculinity. I imagine Susan's delight as she runs her hand gently up my thigh and finds me oh-so-willing inside them... It's no good pretending. I must have Susan. I need her. After all, there's more to marriage than loyalty and parental responsibility. I've tried to discuss it with Gloria over the years but she just says she hasn't found sex exciting or necessary.

So how will I handle this? I could confront Gloria and take the consequences: an angry divorce and half my hard-earned money gone... not to mention my boy's reaction. Would it be worth that?

But then I could marry Susan. I can see her in a silky dress, carrying a bouquet with trailing flowers and a veil half hiding her from my eyes... Or I could have an affair.

That's a very odd term for adultery—with connotations of business and parties. "Black tie affair". Where would we do it? Would we rent some motel room by the hour? You see the signs on some of the motels: "Day rates". I wonder how much they charge. I don't like the idea of skiving off somewhere and doing it in the back of the car. Too uncomfortable and unromantic.

Today I'll give Susan a flower—a red rose of love—before I kiss her.

I gave her the rose. She looked at me warily and thanked me before evading my arms and hurrying towards the office door. She looked so lovely: face flushed, soft lips just begging to be kissed.

But as she opened the door she said calmly: 'How're Gloria and Richard? Are they over that yucky tummy bug yet?'

And when I nodded she shut the door behind her firmly—finally.

What will I do? What can I do? Nothing!

It is 3am. I cannot sleep. I must write.

'Dear Mum,

I'm sorry it has been so long since I emailed you.

Gloria and Richard are almost better now. There's nothing much to report.

The garden is dry and the summer roses are finished...'

A Stroke of Luck

It wasn't as though I hadn't thought things through. I'd planned it right down to the last detail… how I'd have the revenge a lifetime could not assuage; I'd copy the method that Sherlock Holmes used in that story—(what was it called?)—about the nightmares centred around the snake, and the woman who died in terror, and that wouldn't be half of what I'd do to ensure she died—but I must be careful not to let excitement ruin things. I'd read about forensics for example, the DNA, the fingerprints, the strand of hair, the sole of a shoe on a lawn and the lie detector and how it couldn't and I wouldn't be caught by any of that anyhow, since forewarned is forearmed, and I had a timetable that would be foolproof—it was full of alternatives, and my alibi would be unshakeable, and it gave me enormous satisfaction to think how undetectable it all would be and how Annette would suffer, and all because I was so clever and determined and would not be turned away from my purpose, and how revenge was sweet and mine would be the sweetest of all, and how I must remember to tell Annette all about it as she lies there dying, and I must look in the book of quotations and find one that fitted the enormity of death and murder and paying back the pain she'd inflicted on me. Ah, I could see it all now — the shrieks and tears of Annette's family and I would not care — not one bit, and I would laugh privately as they tried to find out how I did it but I would let a crocodile tear slide down my cheek so they were unsure, and couldn't tell what happened was my direction, my one godlike action, and I'd say to them "she was such a good wife and too young to die," and my contentedness would be full...

I laughed in my sleep and this woke me up.

A tear slipped out. I'd never be able to do it now. A week. Is that all it is? It feels much longer. The dreams made it harder. How long was it before I regained consciousness?

I remember every detail of my awakening. I wanted to scratch my nose. I couldn't. Puzzled, I reached over my inert body with my left arm and picked up my right hand. It felt cool and limp — the flaccid handshake of an unenthusiastic politician. No — it was worse than that. It was like shaking a recently dead hand — slightly curled and purplish-tinged — recognisable only by a scar on my index finger. Shocked, I hid it by gently cradling it in the blanket...

I'm paralysed on my right side. Can't speak. I'm incontinent. And Annette is bearing down on my hospital bed now and it's only ten in the morning. The nurse smiles at her as she removes the blood pressure tourniquet from my arm.

'Hello, baby lamb,' Annette mouths a kiss at me. 'Did you have a good night then?' she bellows. She knows I can't answer. 'You know me don't you? Annette, your wife!' She grabs my hand. 'Squeeze my hand, darling — show you love me.' She has my paralysed hand in hers. I'd rather squeeze her throat. She turns to the nurse, pulling a tiny white handkerchief from her handbag as she does so.

'He's no better is he?' She dabs her perfectly dry

eyes. 'It's a week now. Whatever will happen?' The nurse tells her it may be some weeks before they know how much I'll improve. She pats Annette gently on the arm...

Back at my bedside she quavers: 'Could he—will he—die?' Her eyes bore into mine. I glare at her. 'It's all so hard. I don't know what to do. There's the farm...' and she 'cries'. The nurse tries to reassure her. She refuses to be reassured so the nurse leaves to bring her a consoling cup of tea.

When they are alone, Annette firmly grasps my un-paralysed arm with her long fingernails and hisses at me:

'This serves you right. You needn't think I don't know you can hear me and understand. I've been married to you for too long to have the wool pulled over my eyes.' She pulls a chair close to my bed and sits on it, poised for the return of the nurse. God she looks horrible. Her skin reminds me of the tanned hides on one of those ancient peat-bog burials. You know—those murdered heads pre-served in the tannic acid of the bogs. Her breath stinks, even at this early hour, of tobacco and booze. She stays most of the day, drinking tea. The nurses think she's won-derful, but when we're alone her true self appears:

'I'll sell the farm soon,' Annette gloats. 'Move into town and buy myself a nice townhouse or apartment to live in. Then I'll be able to shop and go to the movies and do anything I like. You won't be able to do anything about it! Teach you for being such an old miser. Now you'll be able to think about me spending up large on your money. Give you something to do.' She laughs and leaves.

I must kill her somehow. How? I've got to outlast her—otherwise my Will leaves everything to her. How things have changed since we married in a flutter of con-fetti and lust. How did I imagine she'd fit into life on the farm? Stupid! I might've known by the flashy things she wore and did, that gumboots and haymaking wouldn't do for her.

And children—I wanted a good clutch. I was the

oldest of twelve: nine boys and three girls. Annette didn't want a baby and had her tubes tied to stop that. Now I've no son to carry the family name... My family have owned the farm for nigh-on ninety years. It's a good fertile dairy farm. The best sort of farm. I've got Jersey cows—pure-bred and butterfat. So I must outlive her. I want to leave the farm to my nephew John. He's a reliable keen sort. He'd love the chance to get on that land and he'd never dream of selling it off...

She's back—ready to give me another nightmarish day.

'Just sign these,' she coos. I can't. I'm right-handed. I wouldn't anyway. They look legal. Bugger her. The nurse leaves the room.

'You could write if you tried. You're a naughty boy. Sign or Mummy'll be cross.'

What the hell is this 'Mummy' bit? We've never played that game before.

'Mummy will punish you.' She pinches me on my feeling side, the bitch. I swipe her hand away with my good arm. How she hates me and I hate her. A nurse comes in. Annette sobs.

You can see how it is with us: years of attack and counter-attack. Much of our viciousness up to now has been petty, but it can be infuriating. I mean—listen to her now... The nurse has brought in a menu.

'Tea? Oh, yes. He loves tea—white with two sugars.'

'Black tea,' I scream mentally.

'Now as to the rest—well, he enjoys eggs and bacon for breakfast and lots of meat—but not much in the line of vegetables. He hates those. Just make sure he gets his desserts.' Her eyes are sparkling. She smiles with the small joke and the power she has now. As you might guess, I'm vegetarian. Odd for a farmer, isn't it.

Today's been torture. I crapped in the bed. I couldn't help it. I cried with frustration and anger.

'You've done poos in the bed haven't you—you disgusting old man. You deserve to lie in the mess you've made.' Annette left the room for a while, returning later with calm assurance to call the nurse to clean me up.

'Poor baby,' she coos, and strokes my hair. 'Did you go toilets in the bed then?' I want to grind her face into pulp and smash her. I can't.

I wonder whether she's trying to kill me with my rage just as much as I am trying to plot and kill her... I breathe deeply and survive the day.

Now it's night time. Planning time. There must be some way I can dispose of her. I'm the clever one. Annette's mind runs in simple and predictable ways. That must be an avenue.

She was never popular in Waitara except with a certain class of man. They knew what she'd like. You know — salesmen and the like. They'd take her off in their cars and get her pissed in the local pub. She'd come home with her hair ruffled and her eyes sliding away from mine. I got to be pitied locally. But I'd promised to stay married — 'til death' and all that — and I meant it then. I was a bloody mug.

Must stop all this reminiscing and find a way to be rid of her. It's hard when I'm so crippled. I can't strangle her but savour the thought. I can't imagine how I could get poison or administer it to her. I can't shove her under a train or cut her throat. It'd be best to make it seem as though she'd suicided.

I'm glad I've got this room all to myself. There are no distractions and no witnesses.

Twelve days A.S. (after stroke.) The only word I can say is 'yes.' Anything else I try comes out in a meaningless gabble. I can think sentences but can't say them.

'Yes, yes, yes,' I croak. I sound like a frog. Annette loves that.

'Listen,' she says to her friend Doreen today. 'Listen to that. It doesn't mean anything. It's all he says. He's quite cuckoo. Doesn't understand a thing.' They sit by my bed and peer at me.

'His face is all crooked and his eyes are staring at me,' Doreen whispers. 'Are you sure he can't hear us?'

'Positive. His brain's in a terrible way. Tragic isn't it? He can't even control his waterworks you know—or the other passage. It's awful. The smell sometimes...' She shakes her head.

'Will he recover given time?'

'Oh no! Doctor doesn't believe so. He could linger on for ages like this though.' She sips her tea. 'And it gives me so much trouble. There's the farm. You know what a martyr I've been to that! Years having to help out—and no pay. Not a cent! I'm going to sell it. I'll move closer to town. I'll be able to afford taxis to get around. I never did learn to drive. I'll get some new clothes and so on too. He was always mean with money. He's got heaps stowed away.' She shoots a sharp glance at me, to see if I am listening. I am. That's my new tractor money she's talking about.

'You should use the money, Annette. You certainly deserve it. You won't be able to spend all your days here, either. You'll have to take care of yourself and have some enjoyment.'

'I know,' Annette sighs quite convincingly. 'I know. Do you remember Douglas from the old days? Well, I got in touch with him. He's taking me to a dance tonight. Just to cheer me up of course,' and she sniggers. The morning drags on. I am impotent and enraged.

A.S. plus twenty-three days, I think. (There aren't any calendars here—but at last I have the beginnings of a plan.) I'm stronger on my left side—and generally more alert—but don't let on to anyone. When the doctor asks me to communicate by winking, I just stare blankly at him...'Lights on—no one home,' he mutters to the nurse.

As soon as Annette and I are alone, I mime writing

with my left hand, and point to the magazine she is carrying. She quickly realises what I am trying to do, and gets a pad and pen from her bag. Hurrah for her nosiness. As she holds the magazine up, I laboriously search for the few words I want to 'say.'

'I cannot stand this anymore I do not want to live.'

With increasing interest, Annette writes the words down. She puts the pad on the bed and stares at me before saying with a controlled voice, 'Why don't you kill yourself then?'

'How?' I point.

'Must be some way,' she says thoughtfully. She is trying to restrain herself, but I can see the leap of hope in her eyes. She'd be free if I died: Free to spend up on the trash she loves. I know my solicitor will protect my assets until I die. He knows what Annette's like. Greedy. If only I can die after her everything'll work out OK. I secrete the pad into my bed. She doesn't notice and leaves soon after our 'talk.'

She's now written her suicide note. I hide it in my locker drawer.

Well, that's one step completed—but I still don't know how I'll kill her. The hospital indignities continue. I am catheterised. I loathe it. The days would be unendurable were it not for the urgency of my plan.

A.S. plus twenty-four days. She's back. I listen.

'Did you mean all that yesterday?'

I just stare at her. What does she expect me to do? Recite an impassioned speech of affirmation or denial? Nervously she continues—shooting glances at the door frequently to see if anyone is within hearing distance.

'I went to the library last night.' (That'd be a first!) I looked up—you know—about suicides and helping suicide.' Ah! Is this an offer of assistance?

'I read lots of people kill themselves by overdosing on drugs. I imagine that'd be easy in a hospital. Drugs all over the place.' Imagine is the word! She hasn't a clue. The nurses here bring doses one at a time. They watch me to see when I swallow as if their lives depend upon it. I can hardly leap upon them and steal drugs from the trolley. Is this all the help she can muster?

Her next suggestion is even worse. 'And what about those scapular blades they have? They'd do such damage if you cut yourself.' I want to laugh hysterically. I can't even correct her! Stupid, stupid cow.

Now it's A.S. thirty-five days near as I can remember. Annette is getting impatient with my lack of initiative. Her visits are shorter. Her remarks, when the nurse isn't present, are more pointed. I can see her coming in the door now. Funny—today she looks pleased with herself. She plonks herself on the chair and repairs her lipstick before checking no one is near and then talking to me.

'I have to arrange everything on the farm now you're here. Everything. Mr Miller won't let me have the money I need until a Court approves it. I'm struggling to find enough to eat.' Well, that can't be why she looks smug.

'The possums are a problem again. One of the cows has TB—and John says it's from the possums. He says we'll have to put out bait to kill them.' Aha—I think I can see where this is leading!

Sure enough, Annette pulls some cyanide paste from her bag and asks me to signal if this is the right stuff. I wink at her and am not surprised when she 'accidentally' leaves it behind when she leaves.

I still don't know how I can possibly feed it to her— but it's a great step forward.

About thirty-seven days today. Annette is beside me, dripping with a head cold. Trust her to come and sit close to me—trying to infect me no doubt. A cold could lead to pneumonia and death for me.

'It's all this visiting that's getting me run down,'

she snivels. 'I shouldn't do it—but I can't leave you here alone.' This is for the nurse's benefit.

By now Annette is used to the hospital—and makes her own cups of tea. She's off now—and she's left a cold capsule on the locker. I steal it.

'Could've sworn I took one out of the packet,' she mumbles on her return. She gets another. She doesn't stay long.

Twenty-four hours. At best I've got twenty-four hours to prepare and carry out the plan Annette has unwittingly made. I must empty the capsule and fill it with the cyanide. Her cold won't last long.

Fear threatens to overcome me. If possum bait requires so many grains of cyanide—how much will it take to kill a person? Into my head flies the image of a movie I saw where a sergeant in World War Two was standing in the ruins of a German position and he was searching the bodies for useful bits and pieces—cigarettes and pistols. He showed his mate a capsule that he said the Jerry officers carried to commit suicide. He said it was cyanide—and it was about the same size as the cold capsule—I think. I wonder now whether that was just bunkum.

And what if I poison myself while trying to fill the capsule? It's tiny and slippery and to fill it I'll have to use my one working hand and my mouth... I've got to try. I won't get another chance... Emptying the capsule has gone well. I hold one end between my teeth—being careful not to wet it with saliva or warm it with body heat. It's gelatine. It'd easily melt. Then I pull the other end off and discard the medication into the paper rubbish bag attached to my locker.

Now I have to fill it with the cyanide. I'm terrified— not only about filling the capsule but also sick with fear that a nurse may come in and catch me at it. I rest and try to calm myself while I mentally review the nurses' routine. They check my blood pressure, temperature and so on every four hours. The last check was at one o'clock. It's only one-thirty now by the clock on the wall. But every so often a nurse will come and turn me over to prevent bed-sores. They put the back of the bed up so I am more in a sitting position during the day—and down again at night. I'm buggered if I can work those routines out. I've a feeling they do it between other chores—whenever they can fit it in. Usually around three? Even if there is a routine, it can swiftly change when new patients arrive or any one of a number of things happen. Still, the risk must be taken.

Laboriously I retrieve the jar of cyanide from behind some useless books Annette put in my drawer. It's got a screw cap. Annette's fingerprints will be on the bottle so I must handle it as little as possible. I put a paper towel on the blanket in front of me. I am still scared. I don't want to get it on my skin.

The lid is too tight. My left hand always was my weak hand. I'll put the jar under the blanket and hold it in my groin.

Ah! It's open now. I scrape a small amount of the reddish brown paste onto the paper towel. Thank goodness the capsule is opaque. I'm so frustratingly weak! Look! I'm shaking and sweating and endangering the gelatine again. I've got to rest—just a few minutes rest. Got to slow down the adrenalin... Now—that's better. Picking up one half of the capsule, I push it into the paste and fill it to overflowing. The next step is crucial. I have wiped the outside of the filled capsule as best I can by wiping it on a clean part of the paper towel.

I wedge the cap end under my useless arm and aim the cyanide end towards it. I miss and almost wipe the cyanide on my arm. I'm sweating again. Before I have time to think myself out of it, I try once more. This time! The capsule ends reunite and a new 'cold capsule' is formed.

As fast as I can, I put the paper towel in the bin and hide the jar and the capsule. Not a moment too soon. A nurse has just walked in. I am shaking with the narrowness of my escape.

Thirty-eight days A.S. Annette is late. What if she's too sick to visit me today? What if her cold is better already? What if she's already had her capsule and doesn't take another?

'Hurrah!' I mentally exult as I hear her steps. She's here! She seats herself near my head.

'Still here?'

Obviously.

'Thought you couldn't stand it any more.' She moves restlessly to the window and then returns. 'I'm still sick with the 'flu you know. I don't know why I bother coming.' It is evident that the nurse is not in the room.

'I'll fetch myself a cup of tea.' She comes back with tea and a nurse. The petulant look is still on her face.

'Has he improved—even a teensiest bit?' she quavers. The nurse simply shakes her head. 'Not worse though?' The nurse says I am no worse. Annette looks anxious and depressed. The nurse leaves. Now—if only she'll take a capsule. I have the cyanide on the cool sheets by my left hand.

She is drinking the tea. Is she going to take a capsule or not? How else can I kill her if this plan fails?

She's fossicking in her handbag. For a capsule—or a handkerchief.

'For Christ's sake!' I want to scream. 'Find a bloody pill!' First one then another section of the rubbish-filled bag is being searched. One by one, items are being dumped on the edge of my bed. To think I used to think the untidiness cute in the short days of our courtship! Now I'm almost beside myself as I watch old lolly papers, tweezers, handkerchiefs, bits of paper, an unused sticking plaster, five pens, and other rubbish cascade onto my bed. Has she forgotten to bring the bloody capsules? I'm almost insane with anxiety—but she finds the packet and removes a capsule from the foil.

Now! With my left hand I am sweeping the contents of her bag onto the floor—grabbing the capsule as I do so. Annette is furious.

'Bastard!' she pronounces as she scrabbles on all fours to retrieve her property. 'You did that on purpose.'

Too right. Surreptitiously I swallow her cold capsule and put the cyanide one on top of the blankets. She won't stop carrying on about it.

'Think you're smart....' On and on—until the tea grows cold and I am frantic she won't take the capsule or a nurse may come in to investigate the commotion.

She's sneezing. That reminds her—and she picks up the doctored capsule and swallows it with cold tea. I am not finished.

I flick my bell out of reach. I glare into Annette's horrified eyes as she turns blue and convulses—realising now and at last that I am the victor. She tries to yell my betrayal and call for help but slumps into unconsciousness. Her pulse continues while I get the cyanide paste and her suicide note out of the drawer. I flutter the note onto her body and place the jar into my useless right hand.

Two nurses, too late, walk in. They are responding just as I wish: yelling for a doctor and trying to resuscitate Annette; finding the note and the cyanide. The police come. They talk about Annette's depression when told I hadn't improved and wasn't likely to do so. They don't even notice me at all. They are all assuming my helpless body has a mindless mind....

Yes! I won—and the farm will be safe! The wicked witch is dead!

It's over. I don't know how many days it is now but I'm no longer exultant. I'm not sorry for what I did to Annette. I just want to gloat—to crow—to parade my cleverness to someone: To skite to Annette. But she's dead. The battle between us is over. She was the only one who knew that there was a battle; the only one who knew that inside my silent head is a sentient human being.

They've taken the books—the papers. I tried winking to communicate today. No-one noticed. In any case, I'm afraid to let them know or they may look at Annette's suicide in a new light. My helplessness and boredom are hitting me now for the first time since the stroke: I can't write or read or talk or run across a field chasing a wayward calf. I cannot do anything. Ever.

An uncontrollable scream of laughter and words forces my clenched teeth to open and fills my empty room with sound.

'Yes, yes, yes,' I babble and laugh. I hear the nurses running to me—but I can't stop.

'No one won, no one won, no one won!' shrieks my mind. 'No one won at all.'